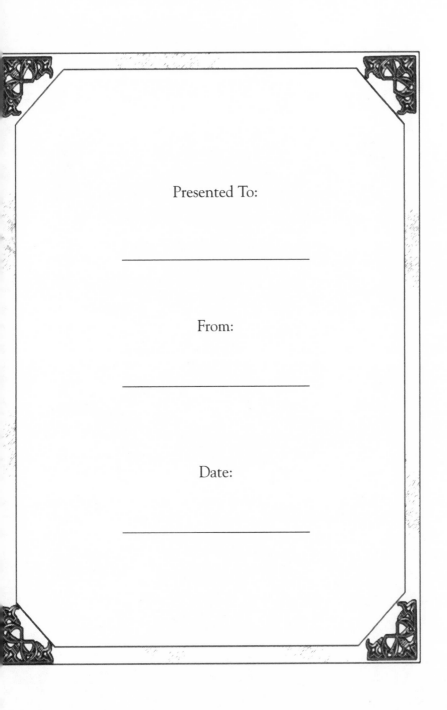

Presented To:

_____

From:

_____

Date:

_____

There seems to be a hunger that drives the soul of man, and

our choices lead us as surely as if we had followed a map.

Some call it luck—whether good or bad.

Others, destination.

From the personal diary of

⤙ Joye Kanelakos ⤚

Jim Stovall

transforming lives together

THE ULTIMATE LIFE
Published by David C. Cook
4050 Lee Vance View
Colorado Springs, CO 80918 U.S.A.

David C. Cook Distribution Canada
55 Woodslee Avenue, Paris, Ontario, Canada N3L 3E5

David C. Cook U.K., Kingsway Communications
Eastbourne, East Sussex BN23 6NT, England

David C. Cook and the graphic circle C logo
are registered trademarks of Cook Communications Ministries.

The Web site addresses recommended throughout this book are
offered as a resource to you. These Web sites are not intended in any way
to be or imply an endorsement on the part of Cook Communications
Ministries, nor do we vouch for their content.

The characters and events in this book are fictional, and any resemblance to
actual persons or events is coincidental.

LCCN 2007930614

Hardcover ISBN 978-1-4347-9990-6
Paperback ISBN 978-0-7814-4547-4

© 2007 Jim Stovall

Cover Design: The DesignWorks Group

Printed in Canada
First Edition 2007

1 2 3 4 5 6 7 8 9 10

061407

INTRODUCTION

I want to thank you for the investment you have made in this book and the message contained in its pages. Time is a precious commodity. I am grateful when people are willing to spend some of it with me in one of my books.

Some of you are beginning this journey with these characters and me for the first time today. Others began the journey through *The Ultimate Gift* book or major motion picture. In any event, I'm glad to have you onboard.

When you turn the last page of this book, I believe you will be a different person than you are right now. This story is about the characters you will read about, but the message is about you and me. This is not a journey or a message for a few hours between the covers of this book. It is a message and a journey for the rest of your life. When you have completed the book, the journey will just be beginning.

As you start your *Ultimate Life* journey, please remember to always share this message and the journey with as many others as possible. Please write to me with your stories of how one of the messages in this book has impacted your life or the life of someone you know. Your words are encouraging to me, and they may just help many others around the world through another *Ultimate Life* book in the future.

Thank you,
Jim Stovall
Jim@JimStovall.com
918-627-1000

This book is dedicated to, as always, Crystal,
who is still the best writer who lives at my house.
It is also dedicated to Dorothy Thompson without whom this book
would not exist, to my professional team that makes me look better than
I should and makes it fun, and to my friends and partners at The
Ultimate Gift Experience and The Ultimate Gift *movie for believing in*
me and the message of The Ultimate Life.

TABLE OF CONTENTS

One | *Life Begins Today* | PAGE 9

Two | *Life Is a Journey and a Destination* | PAGE 21

Three | *The Life of Work* | PAGE 33

Four | *The Life of Money* | PAGE 49

Five | *The Life of Friends* | PAGE 65

Six | *The Life of Learning* | PAGE 79

Seven | *The Life of Problems* | PAGE 95

Eight | *The Life of Family* | PAGE 107

Nine | *The Life of Laughter* | PAGE 119

Ten | *The Life of Dreams* | PAGE 131

Eleven | *The Life of Giving* | PAGE 141

Twelve | *The Life of Gratitude* | PAGE 153

Thirteen | *The Life of a Day* | PAGE 163

Fourteen | *The Life of Love* | PAGE 173

Fifteen | *The Ultimate Life* | PAGE 183

About the Author | PAGE 189

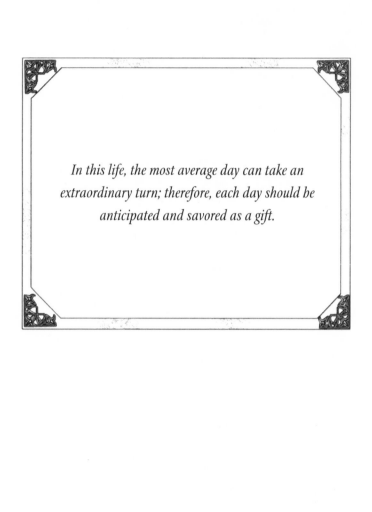

In this life, the most average day can take an extraordinary turn; therefore, each day should be anticipated and savored as a gift.

ONE

LIFE BEGINS TODAY

O bserving the parade of life from my unique vantage point for more than four decades has allowed me to consider the very best and the very worst that humanity has to offer. That particular morning began much like any other. Little did I anticipate or even imagine that it was the dawning of the day that would change my life and the lives of countless others forever.

Sunrise found me, as it generally does, seated at my ornate monument of a desk. These many years I have allowed the outdated and excessive beast to remain, as people who are supposed to know such things assure me that it is befitting my status and a symbol of my chosen lot in life. If the desk is a compromise to my colleagues and position, my chair is an oasis of self-indulgence. It is a custom-made leather creation that, over the years, has expanded and transformed itself to accommodate only me.

I have heard myself described as imposing and overpowering,

among other adjectives. If this is true, it is no doubt a distinct advantage in my chosen profession. Nevertheless, if anything, my legendary leather chair dwarfs even me.

I was attempting to coordinate finishing off the remainder of my second cup of coffee. The anticipated chiming of the historic grandfather clock would announce to everyone up and down the corridor that the beginning of this day would wait no longer. As the majestic clock began to chime ten times, I left the comfortable environs of my chair, traversed around the colossal desk, and made my way toward the ten-foot mahogany door.

"All rise."

I heard the familiar words solemnly intoned that signaled the beginning of my workday.

"Court is now in session. The Honorable Judge Stanford A. Davis presiding."

I stepped through the mahogany doorway, mounted the three steps that rose behind the judicial bench, and settled into my adequate but decidedly less comfortable chair. I gazed out over the assemblage a few beats longer than absolutely necessary, then announced, "You may be seated."

Over the years, I have come to anticipate the gravity or importance of a particular case based on how many participants, observers, and representatives of the media crowd into my courtroom. While not perfect, this barometer has proven itself to be quite accurate over thousands of cases. If it were accurate on this day, I knew that I had never before presided over a case quite like this one.

Each case is unique as the people, situations, and law governing them vary greatly. The law, when adjudicated properly, lies somewhere between a science and an art. A judge must be scientific enough to know the pertinent, repetitive volumes of case law and how they impact every situation while, on the other hand, be artful enough to get into the minds and spirits of those who formed and framed our laws to discern their intent and their lofty ideals as they relate to the modern and current circumstance.

I knew—just as everyone gathered knew, and everyone in the civilized world knew—that the time had arrived for the battle over the estate of Red Stevens. Even though we all recognized this, I stared at the paperwork arranged before me until the courtroom grew deathly silent. Then I pounded my gavel, nodded to my bailiff, and addressed the court reporter.

"The case before the court today is the estate directed by the last will and testament of Howard 'Red' Stevens."

The court reporter's fingers flew unerringly over the mysterious keys just as they had done for many years in my courtroom. I paused reverently, gazing at the counsel and litigants on both sides of the aisle that bisected my marble majestic courtroom.

I knew, in theory, the day I first sat at this bench—and I now know from practical experience—that among the primary roles of a sitting judge is that of appearing, conducting one's self, and acting judicial. When I was first appointed to the bench, I was among the youngest to have ever sat in this position.

I remember commenting to my beloved wife, Marie, that my walk down the corridor each day was intimidating as I had to pass beneath the portraits of all the solemn and wise judges who had gone before me. As a fresh-faced youth, at least in judicial terms, I

felt inadequate to fill their shoes, much less their robes. In the
ensuing forty-plus years when I have expressed my concerns about
my inevitable aging and my own mortality, Marie has repeatedly
admonished me, "You're not getting old, but you are getting very
judicial."

I am ever mindful of the fact that the pomp and circumstance
surrounding the courtroom is not to elevate me but is, instead, to
show the respect and reverence for everything that this courtroom,
as a symbol of our law, represents. I concern myself little with what
people think of me as I live and move and have my being on the
sidewalks and in the streets of our city. But seated here at the
bench, attired in my judicial robes, I become a symbol of all that we
hold dear.

As such, I demand respect—not for Stan Davis, husband,
friend, and neighbor—but, instead, for Judge Stanford A. Davis,
symbol and arbiter of the law.

What can I or anyone say about Red Stevens that hasn't
already been said, written, or broadcast to every part of the
civilized world? Red Stevens was one of those people who became
a legend in his own time and a cultural icon after his death.

Generally speaking, a judge would be called upon to recuse
himself or vacate the bench, turning the case over to another
judge if he had heard as much about the case and the people
involved as I had. Fortunately or unfortunately, there was no
judge anywhere, or person anywhere, who had not heard about
and formed an opinion about Red Stevens, the terms and
conditions of his will, and the case to be presented before me.

Red Stevens was a giant human being in person, reputation,
and deed. His life had been lived so much in the spotlight that it

was hard to separate myth and legend from reality. He had been so famous for so long that his life seemed to have bridged many generations or eras of history.

Red Stevens, as both legend and history tell us, was born into obscurity and unbelievable poverty in the swamplands of Louisiana. As a very young man, he left home headed for Texas with nothing more than the clothes on his back, a head full of dogged determination, and an indomitable spirit full of dreams. Over the next half century, Red Stevens forged an empire in cattle, oil, finance, and industry that rivaled anything the world had ever seen.

Red Stevens did everything in a big way. He was a hard-driving, sometimes ruthless businessman. He was a generous and compassionate philanthropist. He was a valued friend to many and a feared enemy to some. He knew virtually every person of fame and fortune who lived during his time. In many ways, Red Stevens and a handful of people like him defined the twentieth century and established much of what we know as the twenty-first century.

His accomplishments were legendary, but in many ways he was endowed with the human frailties that plague us all. Red Stevens worked unbelievably hard to give his family everything he thought they wanted. Far too late in life, he discovered that mostly what they wanted and needed was him. Near the end of his life, Red Stevens came to realize that, regretfully, he had spent far too much time, effort, and energy at coronations, negotiations, and state dinners and not nearly enough time at Little League games, birthday parties, and family reunions.

He came to this realization at a point in time when he knew he had only a few days or at most a few weeks to live. As he considered the generational dilemma that too much of his money and not enough of his time had created among his relatives, Red Stevens knew that it was too late to help any of his children and most, if not all, of his grandchildren. However, Red in his final days identified what he thought and hoped could be a spark of promise in his young grandson Jason Stevens.

He devised a plan that he executed privately in his last will and testament that became front-page news and popular conversation in every part of our culture. Red left his oil wells, cattle ranches, and financial empire to his children. But, to his grandson Jason, he left through his will a bequest that has become known as The Ultimate Gift.

The Ultimate Gift was a revolutionary idea and was groundbreaking within the field of estate law. It was as unique and special as was Red Stevens. The bequest that Red left to his grandson involved a twelve-month odyssey during which Jason was both encouraged and forced to learn about The Gift of Money, The Gift of Work, The Gift of Friends, and a number of other life lessons. There were a total of twelve gifts that, together, comprised Red Stevens' Ultimate Gift, which he planned for his grandson Jason.

The terms of Red's will called for Jason to learn a real life lesson both through Red's words on video and through tasks Jason was to complete. If Jason successfully completed each task, the will called for Jason to inherit a mysterious Ultimate Gift alluded to by Red Stevens in his will and in the videos he left behind for Jason. Each video message expressed Red's thoughts and experiences pertaining to that individual gift; but the bequest representing Red's Ultimate Gift was never disclosed.

During the year after Red Stevens' death, Jason—under the direction of Red's lifelong friend and lawyer Theodore J. Hamilton—completed to Mr. Hamilton's satisfaction each of the twelve gifts, therefore qualifying to receive Red Stevens' bequest of The Ultimate Gift.

Jason Stevens grew and developed as a person throughout the year, much as a wildflower would flourish that suddenly received the attention of a master gardener. By the time Jason completed the twelfth lesson, which was The Gift of Love, he thought that the lessons themselves were The Ultimate Gift. While this was certainly a major part of Red Stevens' plan for completing The Ultimate Gift, Jason—as a result of accomplishing all twelve tasks—was then directed by Red Stevens' will to receive virtually unlimited control of several billion dollars with which Jason was to help other people experience their own version of Red Stevens' Ultimate Gift.

The seed of an idea that began in Red Stevens' mind was played out as a drama in headlines around the world, and now it had ended up in my courtroom.

On one side of the aisle sat Red Stevens' children and grandchildren who collectively had retained a veritable dream team of high-profile, high-priced lawyers to contest and attempt to overturn Red Stevens' will so they could divide among themselves several billion dollars more than they already had received.

On the other side of the aisle sat Jason Stevens, flanked by one decidedly underwhelming lawyer who, if I had not checked the records, I would have assumed was not old enough or experienced enough to have finished law school. Basically, this looked like a courtroom version of David and Goliath.

Red Stevens' lifelong attorney and friend, Theodore J. Hamilton of Hamilton, Hamilton, and Hamilton, had left the country for an extended sabbatical shortly after Red Stevens' will had been executed and The Ultimate Gift had been presented to Jason Stevens. When last heard from, Hamilton was traveling, lecturing, and studying throughout India and the Far East, and his last communication had come from a remote village in the Himalayas.

The dream team had successfully completed legal maneuvers, freezing all of Jason Stevens' assets, so the totality of Jason's legal firepower in the courtroom before me was embodied in the person of one young Jeffrey Watkins, Esquire. Jeffrey Watkins, my research revealed, had indeed graduated from law school in a somewhat undistinguished manner from a relatively unknown institution of higher learning. As this was virtually his first case, he had no track record to indicate what level of skill or expertise might be hidden behind his unkempt hair, thick glasses, and acne-riddled countenance.

I cleared my throat, waited through a pregnant pause, and then directed my gaze toward the plaintiff's side of the aisle. I inquired, "Are all the parties present and accounted for today?"

An immaculately coiffed and tailored middle-aged member of the dream team rose from the table in front of the Stevens clan. He theatrically gestured, bowed slightly, and spoke.

"Your Honor, if it please the court, I am L. Myron Dudly of the firm Dudly, Cheetham, and Leech appearing before you today representing the rightful and legal claims of the Stevens family, heirs in fact and in law to the estate of Howard 'Red' Stevens."

L. Myron Dudly smiled smugly as muffled applause could

actually be heard from the Stevens family scattered throughout several rows behind him. I pounded my gavel forcefully and sat up straight. I peered over my glasses and down my nose at the lawyer who appeared to have just stepped out of the pages of a gentlemen's fashion magazine.

I growled, "Counselor, you will advise your clients to respect the order and dignity of my court and these proceedings. The court will enter into the record that you are Mr. Dudly of Dudly, Cheetham, and Leech and, further, that you represent the Stevens family in this matter. As to who may or may not be the rightful beneficiary in fact or in law to Howard 'Red' Stevens' estate will be a matter to be decided by this court."

I took three deep and audible breaths and pointed the business end of my gavel toward L. Myron Dudly as I asked, "Do we understand one another?"

Dudly appeared to deflate significantly as he muttered, "Yes, sir."

I set down my gavel and continued.

"Counselor, you can save your theatrics and suppositions for an amateur theater night or game of charades somewhere, but in this courtroom, we deal with facts and law."

Dudly nodded once and dropped into the chair behind him. I think he would have welcomed the opportunity to disappear under the table if the chair had not stopped his progress.

I then shifted my gaze to the other side of the aisle and raised my eyebrows inquiringly. As this elicited no action, I finally had to ask, "Counselor, would you do us the honor of introducing yourself to this court for the record?"

Jeffrey Watkins shakily rose to his feet. His suit had seen better days—I assumed being worn by someone else as it certainly did not fit him. He leaned on the table in front of him as sweat poured down his face. After a few false starts, he finally squeaked out, "Your Honor, I am Jeffrey Watkins representing the defendant, Jason Stevens."

He plopped back into his chair, appearing to have run a marathon as a result of making the one statement before the court.

I was considering the overwhelming mismatch among the legal talent arrayed before me. This was particularly distressing to me as I knew this was going to be an extremely high-profile and complex case with unbelievable assets at stake. Then, without preamble or warning, in one brief instant, the tide turned.

Both of the double doors in the back of my courtroom swung open at the same time. I was reaching for my gavel to admonish my two loyal and long-time bailiffs, Jim and Paul, who knew better than to open the doors while court was in session, when *it* happened.

Out of nowhere appeared an immaculately dressed gentleman who majestically—almost regally—strode down the center aisle of my courtroom. His ebony skin virtually glowed with energy, and the fire in his eyes was evident to all in attendance. As he slid behind the table on the defendant's side of the aisle, he announced what I and every student of the law already knew.

"Your Honor, I am Theodore J. Hamilton of Hamilton, Hamilton, and Hamilton, for the defense."

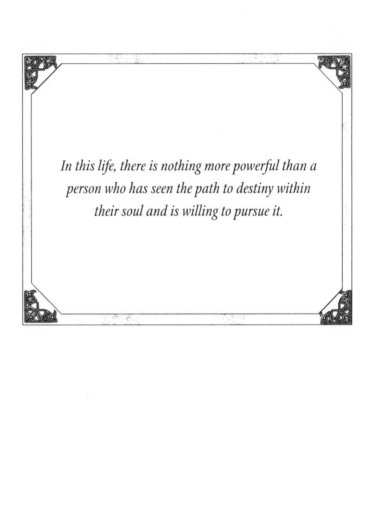

In this life, there is nothing more powerful than a person who has seen the path to destiny within their soul and is willing to pursue it.

TWO

LIFE IS A JOURNEY AND A DESTINATION

The shock of Hamilton's grand entrance reverberated throughout the courtroom. As I pounded my gavel and called for order, I could hear Jason Stevens excitedly exclaim, "Mr. Hamilton, I couldn't reach you. I thought you were lost."

Hamilton smiled wisely and replied, "Young man, there is a vast difference between being lost and simply not wishing to be found."

Before the court could fully come to order, L. Myron Dudly jumped to his feet and declared, "Your Honor, I most vigorously object to this theatrical and disrespectful display exhibited by opposing counsel."

Theodore J. Hamilton slowly rose as the courtroom grew silent. He addressed me but glared across the aisle at Dudly in much the same way that someone would look at an unknown foreign object stuck to the sole of their shoe.

"Your Honor, it was not my intention to upset, intimidate, nor agitate opposing counsel by simply walking into the courtroom."

Mr. Dudly visibly reddened and raised his voice in anger. "Your Honor, I must most vigorously object."

I pounded my gavel for order. I stared sternly at both lawyers then motioned to them as I spoke. "Counsel will approach the bench."

L. Myron Dudly shuffled slightly and then approached the ominous raised judicial bench as if he were a third-grade student preparing to explain how his dog ate his homework. Mr. Hamilton nodded and strode confidently to an area on the polished marble floor directly in front of me. He looked up expectantly.

I certainly knew Theodore J. Hamilton, and he knew that I knew him. Hamilton was nothing less than a legend. When I was in law school and then clerked for old Judge Eldridge, tales of the historic legal exploits of one Theodore J. Hamilton abounded. He had appeared in my court before—always as a consummate professional. He was imposing and intimidating but had the confident aura of someone who knew they had nothing to prove.

Hamilton was like an all-star major-league pitcher. Even though the umpire is trying to be fair, it's hard to call a ball if it's even remotely close to the plate. I glared down at both attorneys.

"Gentlemen, we have a lot of work to do here, and I believe if we will keep the legal matters at hand foremost in our minds and set aside any personal differences, we will be best served."

L. Myron Dudly made the mistake I hoped he would avoid. He spoke.

"Your Honor, Mr. Hamilton seems to think that the rules of law and of this courtroom somehow do not apply to him. We all received ample notice of this hearing to be conducted today and to begin promptly at 10:00 a.m. Maybe Your Honor should instruct counsel in the fine art of telling time."

Theodore J. Hamilton actually chuckled. He paused for an uncomfortable length of time and then he spoke to me while glancing dismissively in the direction of L. Myron Dudly.

"Your Honor, if Mr. Dud—" Hamilton coughed several times, then continued, "—ly ..."

Dudly's eyes actually bugged out as he stammered, "Your Honor, I haven't been referred to as Dud since grade school. I implore you to invoke disciplinary action on opposing counsel for a cheap, demeaning, juvenile gesture."

Hamilton appeared innocent—almost angelic—as he looked up wide-eyed and spoke. "Your Honor, I seem to have developed a tickle in the back of my throat that from time to time manifests itself in the form of a dry cough. It seemed to take hold of me just as I was pronouncing counsel's name, right between the 'Dud' and the 'ly.' I am not familiar with any juvenile antics to which counsel may refer. In fact, as a well-seasoned octogenarian myself, I ask the court's indulgence when my physical ailments from time to time may affect my performance in ways I wish they wouldn't. When Your Honor reaches eighty-plus, I'm sure you will fully understand this."

I heard my always-solemn court reporter, Scott, snicker, and I stifled my own laughter as I responded, "Mr. Hamilton, I have not yet reached eighty, but I am not far behind you, so I do understand your situation; however, the cough did seem to come at a peculiar time."

Hamilton nodded solemnly and said, "Yes, it is quite a curious thing, Your Honor. Unexplainable, actually. And, with regard to my arrival today, I came with all due haste the moment I received word of this hearing."

Dudly interrupted. "Your Honor, our firm received notice of this hearing and copies of the notice received by opposing counsel weeks ago."

Hamilton continued. "Your Honor, I have been traveling extensively throughout India and the Far East on a bit of a sabbatical. Word was forwarded to me as expeditiously as possible by telephone, overnight mail service, facsimile, courier, and finally in the remote regions of the Himalayas via a traveling missionary riding a yak."

Hamilton smiled innocently at Dudly and continued. "Opposing counsel may or may not have any direct experience in executing timely legal documents via yak, but I can assure counsel and Your Honor that a best effort was made by all concerned, and this would, indeed, include support staff, clerks, postal authorities, couriers, the missionary in question, and most certainly the yak himself."

Dudly blurted out, "Your Honor, I am dumbfounded ..."

But all that could be heard was "Your Honor, I am dumb ..." as another coughing fit from Hamilton drowned out the rest.

Dudly pointed violently and continued, "Your Honor, he's doing it again."

Hamilton shook his head disbelieving and solemnly intoned, "Your Honor, when my young, learned, opposing counsel reaches the august age of eighty and beyond, I hope that he will be able to ply his chosen trade without opposition, fifty years his junior, counting and highlighting each time he coughs."

I couldn't help but chuckle as I tapped my gavel for order.

"Gentlemen, let us proceed with the dignity and

professionalism that this court and each of your clients deserves. Please return to your places."

I addressed both attorneys. "Gentlemen, the court will entertain any motions you may have at this time."

L. Myron Dudly stood to his feet and spoke with a recovered sense of dignity.

"Your Honor, this case is a very simple and straightforward one. And when all the evidence has been presented, I am certain that the court will award all of Howard 'Red' Stevens' worldly assets to my clients, in spite of any legal shams or Boy Scout projects that may have been conducted by opposing counsel and his client."

I glanced toward Hamilton, anticipating an objection. Dudly paused as well, assuming he had it coming. Hamilton leaned over toward young Jeffrey Watkins and spoke discreetly. "Son, could you see about getting us some coffee here?"

Watkins replied more shrilly and loudly than necessary, "I didn't go to law school to learn how to get coffee."

Hamilton smoothly responded, "No, I'm sure you didn't learn how to get coffee in law school, but you appear to be a bright youngster, and I have confidence in you."

Hamilton turned toward Dudly as Dudly's motion continued.

"Your Honor, we have filed and this court has granted a restraining order freezing all assets of Jason Stevens that came from Red Stevens either before his death or through that comic book estate proceeding that took place after his death."

I shuffled through my paperwork to locate the pertinent document and responded, "Mr. Dudly, I have that order here before me, and it has been duly executed and recorded. Do you have a point?"

Dudly gestured across the aisle and spoke haltingly. "Your Honor, it's Mr. Hamilton."

I interrupted Mr. Dudly, inquiring, "*What* is Mr. Hamilton?"

At that moment, Jeffrey Watkins scooted back into his seat at the counsel table. He passed a cup of coffee to Jason who slid it over to Theodore J. Hamilton.

Dudly continued, "Your Honor, it is well known in legal circles that Mr. Hamilton charges in excess of 1 million dollars per case, and Mr. Stevens—confirmed by legal audits conducted by our firm—has no financial means of support other than that provided by Red Stevens."

Hamilton looked up as he sipped his coffee and spoke. "Your Honor, if it would be of any help at this point in opposing counsel's motion, I would like to assure the court that I have been adequately retained and promptly paid for my services in this matter; however, I do appreciate Mr. Dud ..."

Hamilton paused to sip his coffee and continued, "...ly being concerned about my fee and my financial well-being."

The courtroom burst into laughter, and I pounded my gavel for order.

Dudly inquired indignantly, "Do you expect this court to believe that you have received your customary compensation from Jason Stevens without benefit of his previous trust or the proceeds from the estate?"

Hamilton smiled, shrugged his shoulders, and stated, "Well, I customarily like to receive a better cup of coffee, but I am willing to accept this one as payment in full for any services rendered or to be rendered in this matter."

I failed to mask my impatience as I said, "If that resolves the issue, I will ask Mr. Hamilton if he has any motions to present to the court."

It was as if an aged boxer came out of his corner for the final round of a championship fight as Hamilton rose to speak.

"Your Honor, I am quite confident that the last will and testament of Howard 'Red' Stevens reflected his intentions and his wishes for his estate. I know this because for more than sixty years Red Stevens was my best friend."

Hamilton paused and continued emotionally, "And, I dare to say that I was his best friend."

Theodore J. Hamilton stopped to collect himself then got down to business. "Furthermore, I can assure this court and all those concerned with this matter that Red Stevens' last will and testament—although informal and somewhat unconventional— was and is valid and binding. I am certain of this as I wrote, filed, and carried out every tenet of the document myself."

Dudly smugly rose to his feet and offhandedly inquired, "Your Honor, does counsel have a point he wishes to make?"

Hamilton fixed Dudly with a stare that would certainly melt a glacier. He paused until Dudly was forced to look away, then spoke.

"I do, most certainly, have a point for opposing counsel and his ..."

Hamilton paused as if searching his mind for the right word to describe something distasteful, then continued.

"... his clients."

Hamilton glanced dismissively at the several rows of greedy relatives arrayed behind Dudly and continued.

"As I do have an intimate personal understanding and

professional working knowledge of Red Stevens' intentions and his will, I want the court to recognize the provision that calls for any relative to lose his or her bequest immediately upon arguing, protesting, or contesting this will or the provisions of Red Stevens' estate."

Hamilton paced back and forth in front of the counsel table. He allowed the bomb he had just dropped to take effect. Scattered murmuring and muttering could be heard from the rows of relatives behind Dudly.

"Lose everything?"

"What does he mean, 'Lose everything'?"

Dudly frantically shuffled through paperwork in front of him.

I tapped my gavel and paused for silence to descend.

"Mr. Hamilton, I have, indeed, anticipated your motion and studied the matter thoroughly. It does appear, without a doubt, that the collected beneficiaries gathered here who have all jointly contested the will have, indeed, forfeited their entire inheritance if this will is upheld."

I heard gasps, curses, and sobs emanating from Dudly's side of the courtroom. I pounded for order and continued.

"Mr. Hamilton, your motion is accepted. It would seem that what we have before us is what my friend and mentor, old Judge Eldridge, called a winner-take-all horse race."

I looked down at Scott typing away at the court reporter's station and said, "For the record, let me state that the court recognizes that if Mr. Dudly and his clients are successful in overturning Howard 'Red' Stevens' will, they will divide all proceeds previously awarded to Jason Stevens. However, if on the other hand Mr. Hamilton is successful in defending the bequest received by Jason Stevens, all other inheritances will be forfeited and be added to the trust currently controlled by Jason Stevens."

The gauntlet had been thrown down. Everything was hanging in the balance.

I rose to my feet, tapped my gavel perfunctorily, and stated, "This court will stand in recess for one hour."

I bounded down the steps, through the mahogany door, and found myself trying to catch my breath in the comfortable, familiar confines of my chambers. Rarely had I considered a case that was this simple yet this complicated. This was magnified as there were billions of dollars riding on my decision.

I paced back and forth for the entire hour, considering Red Stevens' life, his intentions for Jason, and the monumental gifts he had provided for his grandson.

I knew, regardless of any personal feelings I might have, that I had to give every consideration to Red Stevens' children who wanted to inherit even more of his estate. It went beyond more. They, in fact, wanted it all. On the other hand, I had to consider Jason Stevens, as to whether or not he had mastered each of the gifts intended for him and, therefore, might be entitled to several billion dollars. And, finally—after hearing all of the opposing arguments—I had to be the voice of the one person whose wishes were paramount but who was not there to speak for himself. I had to put myself in the mind and heart of Howard "Red" Stevens.

As I took my place in the courtroom and nodded for everyone else to be seated, I noticed two additional figures gathered at Mr. Hamilton's counsel table. Next to Jason I recognized his attractive fiancée Alexia. She had been prominent in all of the media coverage surrounding Jason's Ultimate Gift quest over the last year. And seated next to Theodore J. Hamilton—as she had been in a multitude of courtrooms for almost a half century—was his assistant Margaret Hastings. Miss Hastings is one of those regal beauties who was stunning as a young woman, and the ensuing years have settled upon her like age on a fine wine. If anything, she is more beautiful than ever.

I tapped my gavel, gazed out across the assemblage, and began.

"Ruling on the validity of a last will and testament is among the most critical areas of the law, as it calls upon the court to uphold the rights of an individual and speak on behalf of those individuals who are no longer here to speak for themselves. I have reviewed at length the last will and testament of Howard 'Red' Stevens, including the written documents that contained his thoughts, desires, and intentions as he outlined The Ultimate Gift as a bequest to Jason Stevens.

"This court rules that—having heard no evidence to the contrary or dispute—that Howard 'Red' Stevens was of sound mind and body at the time this last will and testament was created. This court also finds that, although unconventional and quite revolutionary, Red Stevens' will is valid and enforceable if all of the terms and conditions are adhered to and met. Therefore, the only remaining question before this court is to determine whether Jason Stevens has, indeed, accomplished each of the provisions set forth in the last will and testament of Howard 'Red' Stevens."

I paused long enough to let either legal team make any objections they wanted to make. Thankfully, hearing none, I continued.

"The will and subsequent trust documents call for several billion dollars to be given over to Jason Stevens to carry out the mission and the message of the twelve elements of The Ultimate Gift as outlined and presented by Red Stevens. It will be the task of this court to determine whether or not Jason Stevens has, indeed, learned sufficiently each of the twelve lessons to an extent that he would be capable of carrying out the mission underlying those lessons, given the resources represented by several billion dollars.

"Therefore, it is my ruling that beginning at 10:00 a.m. tomorrow morning in this courtroom, we will give Jason Stevens every opportunity to explain and demonstrate that he has learned each of the lessons presented to him by Red Stevens in the twelve gifts; and furthermore that he is up to the task of utilizing several billion dollars to pass on The Ultimate Gift to a world that sorely needs it."

I paused and heard the unbelievable tension created by several billion dollars and countless lives hanging in the balance. I pounded my gavel and announced, "Court is adjourned."

My judicial robes billowed and swirled as I rushed from the courtroom into my chambers. I heard the shock, excitement, and anxiety ripple through the crowd. The overabundance of media present rushed from the courtroom to tell readers, listeners, and viewers around the globe how I had ruled.

I felt somehow unqualified and inadequate to accomplish the daunting task before me. I could only hope and pray that my years of experience on the bench would somehow lead me down the right path and to the proper and just decision.

Only the events of tomorrow and beyond would tell.

In this life, work is the culmination of all we are and all we learn that we bring to others through the marketplace.

THREE

THE LIFE OF WORK

I tossed and turned all night. I could not get my mind away from the case. Every judge in every courthouse throughout the land deals with a voluminous caseload, but in my court and in the minds of people all around the world, the dispute over Red Stevens' estate came to be known simply as *The Case*.

Finally, deep in the middle of the night, I got out of bed, went into my study, and turned on the television. I thought that some mindless TV program might provide escape. As I flipped through the channels, it seemed like everyone everywhere was broadcasting news, commentaries, profiles, conjectures, or tabloid fantasies surrounding Red Stevens, Jason Stevens, and the case.

L. Myron Dudly was prominently featured throughout the media. I had decided early on that this case would unavoidably be a media circus so, instead of trying to control it, I simply let it run its course. But Mr. Dudly was, indeed, making the most of the situation.

———

As the sun reluctantly clawed its way over the horizon and the stars relinquished their domain, another day came to life. I was in my chambers, reclining in the safety and security of my leather chair, nursing my third cup of coffee as I contemplated what had been and what would be. I gazed out of my window at the cityscape.

Most courthouses were built to last. Many are constructed of limestone or marble. They were designed and prominently placed within the center of communities all across the United States. In the ensuing decades, many of these communities have grown toward the suburbs, leaving their courthouses, including mine, in the middle of a blighted inner city.

Outside my window, I could see several vacant, abandoned buildings and several others that should have been vacated and abandoned. There was a barren city block in the middle of it all where sometime in the distant past, bulldozers had knocked down everything that had been there but nothing had ever come along to take root in that place. There had been talk and rumor for as long as I could remember of putting an inner-city park there, but funding and priorities always seemed to be focused elsewhere.

Even though it was several hours before court would be in session, I knew my part of the day's proceedings needed to begin immediately. I removed from the voluminous case file my printed copy of Red Stevens' last will and testament and my DVD copies of the video messages that Red Stevens had made for Jason as a part of The Ultimate Gift.

I selected the DVD marked *The Gift of Work* and put it into the player built into the wall console. This day's court proceedings would be to determine whether or not Jason had accomplished the tasks set forth for him by Red Stevens with respect to The Gift of Work. Furthermore, I would have to determine whether or not Jason Stevens had the ability to apply the lessons learned through The Gift of Work to benefit the world as a result of the enormous trust fund Red Stevens had left behind.

As the DVD player came to life and Red Stevens' imposing face appeared on the screen, I pressed the pause button and stared at the glowing image before me. Howard "Red" Stevens was, indeed, an historical figure. It was hard to separate the truth from the myth and legend. I thought about the emotions and the turmoil that would exist inside of someone who knew they were coming to the end of life, but hoped to leave behind a message after death that they were somehow unable to convey throughout their lifetime.

I pressed "play" and Red Stevens began speaking from beyond the grave to his grandson.

"Jason, when I was much younger than you are now, I learned the satisfaction that comes from a simple four-letter word: *work*. One of the things my wealth has robbed from you and the entire family is the privilege and satisfaction that comes from doing an honest day's work.

"Now, before you go off the deep end and reject everything I'm going to tell you, I want you to realize that work has brought me everything I have and everything that you have. I regret that I have taken from you the joy of knowing that what you have is what you've earned.

"My earliest memories in the swamps of Louisiana are of work—hard, backbreaking labor that as a young man I resented greatly. My parents had too many mouths to feed and not enough food, so if we wanted to eat, we worked. Later, when I was on my own and came to Texas, I realized that hard work had become a habit for me, and it served as a true joy all the rest of my life.

"Jason, you have enjoyed the best things that this world has to offer. You have been everywhere, seen everything, and done everything. What you don't understand is how much pleasure these things can bring you when you have earned them yourself, when leisure becomes a reward for hard work instead of a way to avoid work."

I turned off the DVD player and contemplated the words and the spirit of Red Stevens. I couldn't help but think of my own work life and consider how well I had applied The Gift of Work to my life; but the issue at hand was how much had Jason learned and was he capable of passing on The Gift of Work to countless others around the world.

———————

The courtroom was packed. If anything, the electricity and tension had elevated from the day before. I rapped my gavel and got immediately down to business.

"The matter before this court today is the conditions of the last will and testament of Howard 'Red' Stevens relating to The Gift of Work. The court will decide whether Jason Stevens has proven himself proficient in learning The Gift of Work and, more importantly, if he is qualified to manage several billion dollars in trust to pass on this lesson and gift to others."

I glanced quickly at Theodore J. Hamilton who was calmly taking notes as he listened to my opening remarks. I continued. "Mr. Hamilton, as you are the one who wrote, carried out, and evaluated Red Stevens' last will and testament, the court presumes you find everything to be in order."

Hamilton nodded perfunctorily, and I shifted my gaze to the other side of the aisle. L. Myron Dudly, the rest of the Dudly, Cheetham, and Leech legal team, and the assembled heirs of Red Stevens were in their places. There seemed to be considerably more anxiety present than was in evidence the day before. This was logical as the family previously thought they had nothing to lose and everything to gain, but now they realized that they could quite literally lose it all.

I addressed Mr. Dudly. "Counsel, as your clients are contesting the validity of Red Stevens' last will and testament relating to Jason's completion of the tasks called for, I will let you begin."

Dudly confidently rose to his feet, paused significantly, and then declared, "We call Jason Stevens to the stand."

Jason stood haltingly and tentatively made his way to the witness box. He was seated, and he swore to tell the truth, the whole truth, and nothing but the truth.

Dudly approached the witness box and actually sneered at Jason as he stated questioningly, "You are Jason Stevens?"

Jason nodded and replied sheepishly, "Yes."

Dudly turned to the gallery expansively and said, "Please speak up so everyone can hear you."

Dudly paced back and forth and inquired, "What was the relationship between you and Howard 'Red' Stevens?"

Jason replied cautiously, "He was my grandfather."

Dudly appeared shocked and perplexed. "Are you quite sure he was your grandfather?"

Jason seemed bewildered and repeated, "Yes."

Dudly smiled victoriously and continued. "Can you then please tell this court and everyone assembled why every reference you ever made about Howard 'Red' Stevens, as infrequent as they were, referred to Red Stevens as an obscure uncle or your great uncle?"

Jason reddened and gazed down at his feet. After a long pause, he began. "Howard 'Red' Stevens was my grandfather. He was my father's father. This is something I never appreciated. In fact, I was ashamed of it my whole life until he was already gone. I blamed him for everything that was wrong in my life, and I held him responsible for my father's death. Only after my grandfather was gone did I come to understand that my grandfather was trying to help my father, and my father died as a result of an accident that had nothing to do with my grandfather. Only after receiving The Ultimate Gift am I able to say I am proud to be Red Stevens' grandson and thankful for everything that he taught me."

Jason stared defiantly at Dudly as Dudly continued. "So we are to understand that you feel entitled and deserving of inheriting several billion dollars from someone of whom you were ashamed—and whom you denied being a grandson of—all the years he was alive."

"Yes," Jason croaked.

Dudly smugly looked at the gallery and at me then settled his gaze on Jason and commented, "Shocking. Truly shocking."

Hamilton forcefully interrupted, "Your Honor, I object. Can we please have counsel reserve his opinions and reactions for a time and place more appropriate? Red Stevens' bequests and his reasons for making his bequests are not subject to the approval or the opinions of Mr. Dudly."

I rapped my gavel perfunctorily and sustained the objection in favor of Mr. Hamilton.

Dudly was undaunted and began firing questions toward Jason.

"Have you ever in your life, even once, applied for a job?"

"No," Jason responded.

"Have you ever, even once in your life, held a paying job?"

Jason paused, seeming to think, then shook his head and replied, "No."

"Would you describe for this court and those of us assembled here the brief experience you had at the ranch in Texas last year?"

Jason straightened in his chair and began. "My grandfather taught me The Gift of Work by sending me to work with Gus Caldwell on his ranch."

Dudly smiled and nodded, then inquired, "So, what variety of work experience did you have during that thirty-day period?"

Jason responded, "I dug post holes and built a fence."

"And what else?" Dudly asked.

Jason appeared confused and shook his head, replying, "Nothing else."

Dudly pressed the issue. "So, would it be safe to say that your entire work experience and the totality of your background relating to work is limited to a thirty-day period when you did nothing other than build a fence? Do you feel this, in any way, qualifies you to manage billions of dollars and help other people understand The Gift of Work?"

Jason shrugged his shoulders and stammered inaudibly.

Dudly retreated to his table, exclaiming, "This witness is dismissed. We call to the stand one ..." Dudly paused as he shuffled through his paperwork and announced, "... Gus Caldwell."

It was as if a piece of history or Americana walked down the aisle of my courtroom. Gus Caldwell solemnly put his hand on the Bible and was sworn in. He nodded with respect toward me and Mr. Hamilton.

Dudly barely suppressed a chuckle as he inquired, "So, you are Gus Caldwell."

Gus Caldwell let the silence drag out to an uncomfortable point as only a supremely confident person can do, then replied, "Yes, son, I'm Gus Caldwell. Who might you be?"

Laughter could be heard sprinkled throughout the room. I tapped my gavel for order.

Dudly appeared indignant and replied, "I, sir, am L. Myron Dudly, Attorney at Law, and I am not your son."

Gus Caldwell leaned back in his chair, smiled broadly, and responded, "No, I guess you're not my son. That's just another in the long list of things that I'm thankful to the Almighty for."

The laughter rained down throughout the courtroom, and I couldn't stifle my own chuckle as I pounded for silence and order.

Dudly paused, regained his dignity, and took a different tact.

"Mr. Caldwell, can you describe for this court the nature and extent of your business?"

Gus Caldwell recited the list. "I raise cows, horses. Grow wheat along with a number of other crops. I have oil wells, gas wells, and own parts of banks, shopping malls, and some other stuff I don't know much about."

Dudly nodded as if he understood and continued. "Out of all the tasks, jobs, and positions in all your varied enterprises, can you help us understand the scope and nature of work experience you provided for Jason Stevens?"

Gus nodded and replied brusquely, "He built a fence."

Dudly repeated, "He built a fence. Yes, I see."

Dudly seemed to ponder a moment. "Can you help us understand of what possible benefit thirty days of fence building would be for someone entrusted with billions of dollars for the purpose of helping people, among other things, understand The Gift of Work?"

Gus Caldwell shook his head sadly as if preparing to address a child. "Son, a person who can build a good fence can do anything. The nature of the work is not as important as the nature of the person. Anyone can learn the steps in doing a job, but only a few people understand the pride, the dignity, and the honor that goes with doing a job well. My outfit has grown to be worth a lot of money, and I'm able to handle it all, and I never got that out of a book. I guess I learned a lot about work and a lot about life from hard labor like building miles of fence."

Dudly shook his head, as if he and everyone else in hearing range would be disappointed in the answer, and retreated to his counsel table stating with a dismissive wave, "Your Honor, I believe we have learned all we can and will from this witness."

Gus Caldwell looked up at me questioningly, and I smiled

and nodded, saying, "Mr. Caldwell, the court thanks you for being here today."

Gus rose and replied, "Sir, you don't need to thank me. I'd do anything you can imagine and some things you can't for Red Stevens."

Gus Caldwell walked down the aisle and out of my courtroom with every eye riveted on him.

Eventually, I turned my gaze back to Dudly and inquired, "Mr. Dudly, have you other witnesses?"

"No, Your Honor," he replied. "I believe we've heard more than enough from Mr. Caldwell and Mr. Jason Stevens himself to understand that this young man ..." Dudly jabbed a finger in Jason's direction as he spoke "... does not and could not know anything about the world of work even as it relates to himself, much less the ability and understanding to manage billions of dollars to help others."

I sat back in my chair and stared at Mr. Dudly as I pondered the situation.

Then Hamilton rose to speak. "Your Honor, the matter before the court is not Mr. Dudly's opinion of Red Stevens' will or even Mr. Dudly's opinion of Jason Stevens' work habits. The matter before the court is quite simply, does Jason Stevens understand The Gift of Work and can he pass this lesson on to others through the resources left by his grandfather. I believe—and his grandfather's wishes demand—that he be given a chance to prove his worthiness in this matter once and for all."

Hamilton sat down as if the matter was decided and, indeed, the matter was decided. My eyes settled for a moment on each lawyer in turn, and then I ruled.

"It is the decision of this court that Jason Stevens be given thirty days to prove, by his own means and in his own way, that he understands The Gift of Work and that he, indeed, possesses the wherewithal to pass along Red Stevens' Gift of Work to others. If at the end of thirty days the court is satisfied in this matter, we will proceed to the next gift. If not, the last will and testament will be overturned, and the assets of the Red Stevens' Trust shall be divided pro rata among the heirs who are a party to this suit.

"Court is dismissed."

——— ———

The media coverage in the ensuing days was relentless and unprecedented. Dudly, Cheetham, and Leech got a lifetime worth of face time while Hamilton must have found a place to hide from the media. Jason Stevens' sightings were recorded here and there with questionable reliability. Frankly, we were all in the dark.

I wondered if I had done the right thing, considering Jason Stevens and, more importantly, Red Stevens. Was this task reasonable, and was it even possible?

I handled the rest of my caseload for the next few weeks and tried to focus on other matters.

——— ———

Then an unforgettable day came. As usual, I was sitting in my leather chair with my cup of coffee as the morning first became a hint then a reality, when I observed a sight my mind simply wouldn't register. My normal view out the picture window of my chambers showed the sun rising in the east just as it should, and showed the abandoned buildings and the rundown tenements. It showed the vacant block where the bulldozers had left their mark, but something—in fact, everything—was different both in spirit and in practice.

As the day had barely begun, I observed a Texas-style rail fence materializing around the previously vacant block. Neighborhood youth, actually gang members, were swarming all about the area performing a variety of tasks—some of which were clear to me, while others remained a mystery.

As the day matured, the climbing sun revealed delivery trucks unloading building supplies and playground equipment. Merchants, business leaders, and residents of the area clustered in groups around the perimeter, and several television trucks appeared to cover the unfolding events.

Deep down, I suspected what was happening. I smiled and then laughed out loud in the privacy of my chambers. I simply couldn't wait for the approaching day in my court when the reality of the situation would be exposed.

I greeted everyone gathered in the courtroom as I tapped my gavel for order.

"Good morning. The purpose of this hearing is to make a final determination regarding Jason Stevens' completion of tasks and suitability for responsibilities with respect to the last will and testament of Howard 'Red' Stevens. The court will ask Jason Stevens to take the stand."

Jason moved confidently to the witness box, was eagerly sworn in, and sat on the edge of the chair. I nodded toward Mr. Hamilton to proceed.

Hamilton casually sat at the counsel table, glanced up at Jason, and said, "Jason, why don't you tell them what happened."

Jason paused, took a deep breath, and began. "Well, in all of my trips into and out of the court building last month, I had to walk past that vacant block down the street. I heard a number of people throughout the area comment on how, for years, they had wanted to have a park there. Apparently there had been petitions, fund drives, demonstrations, and lawsuits, but nothing had ever happened.

"My grandfather taught me, through his words and through his life, the power of someone with a vision who is willing to simply go to work.

"After court was dismissed last month, I went over to that vacant land and, among the rubble, found a number of old wooden utility poles. I just got some tools, cut up those poles, and did the only thing I knew how to do. I started building a fence around the vacant land. Then kids, teenagers, retired people, and all sorts of others began showing up and asking what I was doing. I let them know that this was going to be a park if we were all willing to believe it and simply work for it. I told them we didn't need the government, or a bond issue, or a lawsuit or a demonstration. We just needed a big dream and a little work.

"While I kept building the fence, some kids started cleaning up the area. Local business leaders made arrangements to have grass planted and trees put in. Several contractors used concrete left over from other projects to build sidewalks and a parking lot. And, well ..."

Jason paused meekly and looked up at me and said, "Your Honor, I think if you'll walk over there, you'll notice that we got a park."

Applause rippled throughout the courtroom. I reached for my gavel to call for silence but decided it could wait a few moments while the applause continued.

I smiled at Mr. Hamilton then down at Jason as I spoke.

"Let the record show that it is the finding of this court that Jason Stevens has demonstrated not only his understanding of The Gift of Work but his uncanny ability to pass it on to others. We will take up the matter of the next gift, being The Gift of Money, at 10:00 a.m. tomorrow. This court is adjourned."

Money is the fruit of our efforts and
the fuel for our dreams.

FOUR

THE LIFE OF MONEY

I enjoy a brisk walk, watching a sunrise, and being in a pleasant park. The next morning, I was doing all three at the same time. There is something about watching the sun perched on the horizon that brings an emotional punctuation to the day.

My beloved wife, Marie, shares my sentiments regarding observing the sun on the horizon. However, she feels that the sunset is more in tune with her schedule than the sunrise.

The air felt crisp and clean that morning in the park. It wasn't just any park. I was walking in the new Howard "Red" Stevens Urban Park as the sign at the entrance had proclaimed. The sign also informed me, and anyone else entering, that "This park is dedicated to and provided by the hard work of people in this community."

The sunrise was magnificent from my park perspective. I was just a mere stone's throw from the courthouse. In fact, I could see the sunrise reflecting off the picture window in my chambers;

however, I was struck with how a different view can entirely change one's perspective on the world. This seemed to me to be a good thing for a judge to keep in mind, both figuratively and literally. Often, judges are forced to use the law and their intellect to come to a decision that is opposed to the ruling their heart wants them to make.

I settled onto a park bench and observed, among other things, a rather fit young lady wearing some type of space-age form-fitting jogging suit, making her way around the perimeter of the park followed closely by her dog. The dog was some kind of Labrador-terrier mix. When the pair reached the open space in the park across from me, they stopped, apparently having completed their route.

The young woman reached into a backpack and took out a tennis ball. She threw it a short distance, and her dog leapt into action, retrieved the ball, and brought it back to her. She repeated this process several times as I casually looked on. Then she reached into her backpack and withdrew several more tennis balls. This time when the dog returned, she threw out two tennis balls. The dog was quite skilled and was actually able to get both of them situated in his mouth and bring them back to the young woman.

But then she threw out four tennis balls. The dog ran eagerly toward the cluster of tennis balls. He frolicked about excitedly like a child in a candy store, having four tennis balls to retrieve; however, his best efforts repeatedly failed as he tried to get all of the tennis balls in his mouth at once.

As I enjoyed this process from afar, I couldn't help but allow thoughts of the Stevens' case to enter my mind. Overnight, I had watched several news reports that featured Mr. Dudly with Red Stevens' son Jack in tow. I was struck by the fact that Jack Stevens had inherited several hundred million dollars, but somehow it wasn't enough. He was risking losing it all because he wanted more.

The dog grew more frustrated and agitated as each time he would pick up one or two of the tennis balls, they would slip from his mouth as he tried to retrieve a third one.

As I rose from the park bench and began making my way toward the courthouse in the distance, the dog became so frustrated he ran in circles, howled, and rolled over onto his back with all four paws in the air.

As I passed him, I told him, "You remind me of some humans I know."

He cocked his head and moaned. Somehow I don't think he appreciated the comparison.

I waved at the young lady and smiled as I passed. She pointed at her dog and said, "Sometimes he's not too bright."

I chuckled and replied, "Well, it happens to the best of us."

I was looking forward to having dinner that night with Marie at one of our favorite restaurants. I somehow knew she would be really fascinated with the lesson I had learned from the attractive young woman in spandex and her dog. But I had a day in court with many miles to go before my dinner with Marie.

———

"All rise," Paul, my bailiff, somberly intoned as I climbed the familiar three steps and settled into my place. I gaveled the proceedings to order and organized my thoughts.

I had hoped that counsel for the Stevens' family might let my previous day's ruling stand without protest or objection, but I didn't have much confidence in that happening.

"Your Honor," Dudly beckoned.

I glared at him and inquired, "Yes, what is it?" as I began to realize my fears.

He replied, "We have a number of objections and motions that justice and the gravity of this case require us to make."

I nodded, accepting my fate.

He continued. "Your Honor, first and foremost, we object to Mr. Stevens' escapades in the park being ruled as actual work, pertaining to The Gift of Work as outlined in Red Stevens' will documents. Jason Stevens received no money or other remuneration for his efforts; therefore, we believe that he did not do any work, nor does he have the ability to guide others utilizing Red Stevens' Trust to understand and accomplish their work. For the purposes of this matter, having not earned any money, Mr. Stevens' efforts are worthless."

Mr. Hamilton cleared his throat and made an offhanded comment from his seat. "Your Honor, if not earning money through work makes someone worthless, Mr. Dudly's clients would, indeed, have to be ruled worthless. We believe Red Stevens' desires were very clear and that Jason Stevens far exceeded the requirements of the will."

I nodded toward Mr. Hamilton and replied, "I would have to agree with you, Mr. Hamilton."

I shifted my gaze toward Mr. Dudly. "Objection overruled."

Dudly turned the next page in what appeared to be an ominously lengthy document.

He continued. "Your Honor, we further object to Mr. Stevens' unauthorized, unethical, and indeed illegal activities that he somehow has come to call an urban park."

Mr. Dudly intoned the words *urban park* as if they were somehow distasteful and beneath him.

My patience was growing thin. I pointed my gavel at him and said, "Counselor, if you have a point in all this, I would like you to make it now."

L. Myron Dudly reddened slightly and cleared his throat. He knew he was on very thin ice, but he collected himself and waded in.

"Your Honor, Mr. Jason Stevens would have to obtain building permits, city and county right-of-way zoning variances, and deal with employment issues as well as child labor laws in order to have appropriately conducted his activities over the past month. Furthermore, his trust fund and the proceeds of the estate have all been frozen, and as Mr. Hamilton is working apparently for a fee involving a cup of coffee, there are obviously a number of financial irregularities, if not downright illegal misappropriations, involved here."

Theodore J. Hamilton forcefully cleared his throat and ponderously rose to his full height.

"Your Honor, if you will allow me, I may be able to clear up all of the fog created by Mr. Dud—"

Hamilton experienced one of his brief coughing fits and did not even bother to complete the second syllable of Mr. Dudly's name.

Dudly rocketed to his feet and pounded his clenched fist on the counsel table.

"Your Honor, how long must I suffer these indignities?"

Hamilton looked at Dudly innocently and said, "I'm the one suffering the cough here. Are you experiencing any ailments, counselor?"

Dudly's face achieved the color and hue of one of my beloved sunrises.

Hamilton stated with dignity, "May it please the court, I beg Mr. Dudly's indulgence with regards to any annoyance created by my advanced years."

Dudly shot back, "When I get to be eighty, I can assure you I won't be annoying people in the courtroom."

Hamilton smiled beneficently and announced, "Mr. Dudly, I believe we can all agree you won't have to wait till you're eighty as you have adequately and repeatedly demonstrated your vast ability to annoy people now."

Mr. Dudly's face achieved an even brighter sunrise coloring as he dropped into his chair in frustration.

I pounded my gavel for order, and the courtroom finally grew silent once again.

Hamilton spoke. "Your Honor, I am hoping we can avoid wasting the court's time with each minute detail. I am prepared to stake my reputation as a member of the Bar for well over half a century that the zoning permits, easements, variances, work permits, and all other state, county, and municipal documents are in order and have been duly filed. I can assure the court of this as it was handled most expeditiously by the law firm of Hamilton, Hamilton, and Hamilton."

Dudly whined, "What about the money? Where did all of the funds come from for that so-called park?"

Hamilton smiled magnificently and, with a gleam in his eye,

proudly stated, "Yes. Thank you for bringing that to the court's attention and my recollection. There was, indeed, a generous donation made to the newly formed Community Urban Park Fund."

Mr. Hamilton paused opportunely, shuffled through a stack of papers, found the one he apparently had been seeking, and continued as he slipped on his antique reading glasses.

"Yes, here it is. A registered letter, duly signed and notarized, accompanied by a cashier's check made out to the Community Fund."

Dudly interrupted. "Your Honor, I object. Would you please direct counsel to reveal the source of the so-called funds?"

Hamilton indignantly continued after glaring at Dudly.

"Thank you, counselor. I was just getting to that prior to your last eruption. Although the benefactor wished to remain low profile, if not indeed anonymous, I have been authorized to reveal to the court that all outstanding expenses required to complete the Howard 'Red' Stevens Urban Park were donated by a newly formed organization."

Hamilton adjusted his glasses and peered at the document he held.

"This newly formed organization is known as the Alpine Texas Fence Builders Corporation. Your Honor, the ownership of this newly formed corporation seems to be covered by a number of trusts and shell corporations, but I can assure the court that the corporation itself, and the funds received for the Community Park, are legal and well accounted for."

Dudly lowered his head onto the counsel table in front of him. The other members of the Dudly, Cheetham, and Leech team seemed perplexed and agitated. Grumblings and mutterings could be heard from the assembled Stevens clan arrayed in the rows of seats behind Mr. Dudly.

I let the silence draw out for several moments and spoke.

"Hearing no other motions or objections, I believe we can press on with today's business before the court. Today with respect to Red Stevens' last will and testament, we will be hearing arguments surrounding Jason Stevens' response to The Gift of Money portion of The Ultimate Gift as well as the court's findings with respect to Jason Stevens' ability to manage several billion dollars in Red Stevens' Trust to benefit society relating to The Gift of Money."

I gestured toward Mr. Hamilton.

He responded as a matter of fact, "Your Honor, we are satisfied that Jason Stevens did, indeed, perform sufficiently regarding The Gift of Money, and he is, therefore, qualified to manage the trust as outlined in the last will and testament of Red Stevens."

My gaze had barely settled on Mr. Dudly when he spoke. "Your Honor, we call Jason Stevens."

Jason was seated in the witness box, and I informed him and everyone present that he was already sworn and would still be under oath with regard to his testimony in the matter.

Dudly began. "Mr. Stevens, have you ever earned any money in your entire life?"

Jason shook his head slowly.

Dudly bore in, saying, "Please answer the court."

Jason said, "No."

"Have you ever managed or invested any money?" Dudly inquired.

"Not really," Jason responded.

"Then can you please tell this court how any reasonable person could trust you to earn and manage your own money, much less several billion dollars that should rightly be inherited by my clients?"

Dudly gestured to the assembled relatives on his side of the courtroom.

When Jason did not answer, Dudly shrugged and commented, "Well, I guess we have our answer. We have no further questions."

Hamilton approached Jason. "Jason, isn't it true that after you spent a month in Texas building a fence for Gus Caldwell, that you were given a certain amount of money as directed by your grandfather's will?"

Jason replied, "Yes, I guess they figured that I would have earned about fifteen hundred dollars for that fence I built, so I was given that much and told to go out and find people whose lives could be helped by the money."

Hamilton nodded and said, "So, what did you do then?"

Jason gazed off into the distance as if remembering a different time and place, and then he spoke as if recalling a fond memory.

"Well, first I found a group of Scouts who were two-hundred dollars short in their fund-raising to go to their Jamboree. Then a woman with a baby was having her car repossessed, and I gave her four hundred dollars to keep her car. Next, I found a family shopping in a toy store. The parents told the children that Santa would not come this year. When the children were in another area of the store, I gave the parents three hundred dollars to make sure Santa would make it to their house. Next, I found an old lady sitting on a bench crying because she didn't have the money to buy her husband's heart medication."

Jason paused and looked up at me. There were tears in his eyes as he continued.

"They'd been married fifty-seven years, and she told me they had never missed a payment in all those years. I gave her two hundred dollars, which would cover three months of the heart medication with twenty dollars left over for her to take her husband, Harold, out to lunch at his favorite place. And last, I discovered a car broken down at the side of the road where I met a young man named Brian. He needed his car to get back and forth to work or he was going to lose his job. The mechanic said it was going to be seven hundred dollars, so I gave him the money."

Hamilton smiled as if looking at a son of whom he was most proud. Hamilton glanced up at me and then out at the gallery and said, "I believe that meets the terms and conditions of Red Stevens' will."

Dudly sprung to his feet and said, "Your Honor, we object."

He was holding an adding machine tape dangling from his left hand. One of the Dudly, Cheetham, and Leech clerks at the end of the counsel table actually had an adding machine in front of him.

Dudly smirked defiantly at Hamilton and stated, "Your client was directed to spend fifteen hundred dollars but claims to have spent eighteen hundred. This points out the fact that Jason Stevens cannot take care of his own money, much less billions of dollars which my clients are lawfully entitled to."

I glanced over at Mr. Hamilton.

He responded, "Jason, can you explain the three-hundred-dollar discrepancy in this matter?"

Jason seemed at a loss and spoke. "Well, he really needed the car, and it cost seven hundred."

Hamilton continued. "So where did the other three hundred dollars come from?"

Jason seemed nervous but spoke forcefully. "I got the three hundred out of my pocket."

Dudly blurted out, "I object. Obviously, this does not meet the criteria set forth by Red Stevens. He was to distribute fifteen hundred dollars and, in doing so, demonstrate he could manage money. I don't find that he accomplished this."

I pounded my gavel and ruled, "Well, I do find that he met both the spirit and the letter set forth in the document, and if during the next thirty days Jason Stevens can demonstrate he can pass along The Gift of Money to others, this portion of the case will be duly resolved. Court is adjourned."

Back in my chambers, Red Stevens spoke to me from the DVD just as he had spoken to Jason about The Gift of Money.

"Today, we are going to talk about what may, indeed, be the most misunderstood commodity in the world. That is, money. There is absolutely nothing that can replace money in the things that money does, but regarding the rest of the things in the world, money is absolutely useless.

"For example, all the money in the world won't buy you one more day of life. That's why you're watching this videotape right now. And it's important to realize that money will not make you happy. I hasten to add that poverty will not make you happy either. I have been rich, and I have been poor—and all other things being equal—rich is better.

"Jason, you have no idea or concept of the value of money. That is not your fault. That is my fault. But I am hoping in the next thirty days you can begin to understand what money means in the lives of real people in the real world. More of the violence, anxiety, divorce, and mistrust in the world is caused by misunderstanding money than any other factor. These are concepts that are foreign to you because money to you has always seemed like the air you breathe. There's always more. All you have to do is take the next breath.

"I know that you have always flashed around a lot of money and spent it frivolously. I take the responsibility for this situation because I deprived you of the privilege of understanding the fair exchange between work and money."

They were lined up along the wall, shoulder to shoulder, across the back of my courtroom. They were lined up along either side of the gallery from the back of the room to the front. There were three sides of a perimeter made up of all shapes, sizes, and descriptions of young women.

A month had come and gone quickly since I had sent Jason Stevens out to prove himself regarding The Gift of Money. I had called the court to order and, like everyone else present, was curious about the gathering of young women, but before I could make any inquiries, predictably, Dudly spoke.

"Your Honor, I object. What kind of outrageous display or grandstanding tactic of opposing counsel is this?" Dudly gestured to either side then behind as he continued. "My clients and I would like to know the meaning of this."

I shrugged and commented, "I would like to know the meaning of this as well."

Hamilton chuckled and spoke. "Your Honor, I know the meaning of this but feel it would be best explained by my client."

Jason took the stand. Hamilton approached as he asked, "Jason, would you like to inform everyone about the gathering of young ladies lined up around the courtroom today?"

Jason smiled shyly and replied, "I didn't tell them to come here."

Dudly blurted out his objection. "Your Honor, are we to believe that Jason Stevens had nothing to do with this gathering?"

Jason continued as he glanced up at me. "Well, I know who they are, and I know why they're here, but I didn't tell them to come."

Hamilton encouraged Jason, asking, "Can you tell us, then, who they are?"

Jason looked at the ring of young ladies around the room and began. "I heard in a news story that single mothers are among the most financially disadvantaged people in our society. So I went around in some low-income areas—through day-care centers, schools, community centers, and low-income housing—and found a number of single moms. I asked them about their specific needs, and ..." Jason seemed to struggle for the right words.

"Well, I guess we came up with sort of a program."

Hamilton smiled and asked, "Can you tell us about this program?"

Jason continued. "Well, the first and biggest problem seemed to be that they are spending a lot of money on day care, and they don't have enough time with their kids. So we came up with a day-care co-op where the mothers take care of one another's children while they're trading off working day shifts, night shifts, and weekends. This gives them more time with their kids and saves a lot of money on day care."

Hamilton nodded for Jason to continue.

"Next, we got them all wills, guardianship power of attorney documents, and all of the things that single moms running a household would need. We helped them shift high-interest credit card debts to lower interest cards, and a lot of them just got rid of credit cards all together. We've started financial classes where we bring in volunteer experts from the community to help them learn about managing money and moving ahead in their careers and lives."

Hamilton was beaming. He gave a thumbs-up gesture to Jason, turned, and actually bowed to Mr. Dudly, announcing, "Your witness, Counselor."

Dudly stalked Jason, who leaned back in his chair defensively. Dudly attacked. "Mr. Stevens, what if anything qualifies you to help these young women or anyone with legal documents, credit problems, or financial planning?"

Jason shrugged and said, "Really, nothing at all. Mr. Watkins and Miss Hastings helped out."

Jason nodded toward the counsel table.

Dudly glared up at me and declared, "Your Honor, Jason Stevens didn't help anyone with money. He got other people to do it for him. He's simply not qualified to ..."

The pounding of my gavel interrupted Mr. Dudly.

"Mr. Dudly, it is a long-recognized fact in our society that people who need to accomplish complex or specialized tasks seek the expertise of others. This is why firms such as Dudly, Cheetham, and Leech exist."

I gazed at the long line of young ladies ringing my courtroom. They were clean and presentable, but the cost of their combined wardrobes would not have paid for one of the outfits worn by the Stevens clan seated behind Dudly. But the women somehow seemed to have a pride and dignity I couldn't quite define. Maybe it was simply hope.

I looked down at my court reporter, Scott, and stated, "Let the record show that Mr. Stevens has duly and admirably completed all tasks to this court's satisfaction with regard to The Gift of Money."

A hearty cheer rose from all sides of my courtroom. I couldn't bring myself to pound my gavel for order.

I looked at Hamilton and Dudly, in turn, and declared, "Gentlemen, tomorrow is another day. Court is dismissed."

No one can be considered a failure who has a friend, and no one can be considered a success without one.

FIVE

THE LIFE OF FRIENDS

The media coverage that I hoped would die down was, instead, accelerating. Images of the young single mothers lined up around my courtroom were inescapable on television and in the print media.

I sought legal precedent for high-profile cases of this nature that would be carried out over an entire year or more. Unfortunately, there was no precedent, so I had the dubious honor of breaking new legal ground.

One of my favorite nightly news interview programs featured Mr. Dudly and Red Stevens' younger son Bill. The program captured my attention before I could change the channel.

Bill first stated innocently that this case wasn't about the money. Along with phrases like "The check's in the mail" and "I'm from the government, and I'm here to help you," the phrase "It's not about the money" must be prominent in the Liar's Hall of

Fame somewhere. More than four decades on the bench have taught me "It's always about the money."

The host of my favorite nightly news interview program failed to press Bill on the money issue and let him ramble on about what a worthless, irresponsible playboy Jason Stevens had been his whole life and how the rest of the family was regrettably forced to come together to fight Jason in court so that they could each receive their legitimate inheritance.

Bill explained, "Depriving rightful heirs of the fruit of our beloved father's efforts—to give it over to someone like Jason—simply cannot be allowed, no matter how much time and money it takes to stop this injustice."

The host asked, "Bill, are you concerned that you've lost the first two phases of this twelve-step case?"

Bill waved his hand dismissively and quipped, "No, it's no big deal, because it's like we have twelve hurdles. Jason and his old lawyer have to get over all twelve of the hurdles in order to win. We, the rightful heirs, only have to win one hurdle in order to get our inheritance."

As the program was drawing to a close, the host inquired, "Mr. Stevens, are you concerned that if you lose this case you not only don't get Jason Stevens' portion of the estate, but you lose everything you had previously inherited? Wouldn't this leave you and your family penniless?"

Bill chuckled nervously. The hot TV lights seemed to be causing him to perspire at that very moment. He cleared his throat and croaked, "We are very confident, with the able help of Mr. Dudly, that justice will be served."

The theme music for the show began playing, signaling the

end of the program. The interview had reminded me that it was, indeed, a long road ahead with many potential hazards along the way. And Jason's position reminded me that the hunter can make many mistakes but the hunted can make only one.

———————

My bailiffs, Jim and Paul, stopped me in the corridor. We didn't get to speak very often considering that we worked in the same room all day, every day.

Jim blurted out, "We're sorry."

I must have appeared not to understand as Paul explained, "We should have done something about those women or told you before court began."

I patted them both on the shoulder and said, "Gentlemen, it's a public building and an open court. No explanations necessary."

I laughed as I voiced my thoughts. "Somehow, I fear the atmosphere will be lacking in the courtroom today."

Indeed, as I entered the courtroom and took my place, although the courtroom was packed, the long line of young women was no longer in evidence. It had been a sight I would not soon forget.

I rapped my gavel, took a deep breath, and began. "Today, we will be exploring The Gift of Friends."

I looked at Theodore J. Hamilton and inquired, "Counselor, are you prepared?"

I smiled to myself as I thought, *Asking Theodore J. Hamilton "Are you prepared?" is like asking a hungry lion if he would like to eat.*

Hamilton simply nodded, and Jason took the stand.

Then, Hamilton inquired, "Jason, would you tell the court what you learned from your grandfather about friendship?"

Jason licked his lips, took a deep breath, and began. "I had never understood the real definition of a friend or the depth of friendship before my grandfather gave me The Gift of Friends."

Jason seemed to be struggling with his thoughts as Hamilton nodded for him to continue.

"I guess a friend is someone you can count on, no matter what happens. They applaud the best things you do and accept the worst things you do."

Hamilton proceeded, "During the month that Red Stevens taught you about The Gift of Money, you went out and met someone that you had never been introduced to before, and you subsequently became friends."

Jason nodded and said, "Yes."

Hamilton continued, "Are you still friends to this day?"

Jason nodded and said, "Yes. We don't talk as often as we'd like, but we are friends."

Hamilton looked up at me and said, "Your Honor, I believe this does accomplish everything Red Stevens set forth in The Gift of Friends. There is simply nothing more or less required of a friend."

Mr. Hamilton returned to his seat as Mr. Dudly inevitably rose. "Your Honor, if I may."

I nodded at the unavoidable situation.

Dudly continued, "We have a few questions. Jason, you reportedly met a young man named Brian when you were asked to demonstrate The Gift of Money."

Jason nodded and replied, "Correct."

Dudly smiled conspiratorially and asked, "Would you please

tell the court the circumstances under which you met Brian and how you became friends?"

Jason shrugged and began. "I was driving away from Mr. Hamilton's office after I had watched the video made by my grandfather telling me about The Gift of Money. His words and examples had really affected me. Then I noticed a car stalled at the edge of the road. I pulled over, and that was how I met Brian. I helped him get a new engine, and we began to talk and do things together, and now we're friends."

Mr. Dudly laughed out loud and said, "Let me get this straight. You found someone broken down at the side of the road, you bought him a new engine, and you think you have a friend."

Jason nodded and stared directly at Dudly, replying, "Yes, sir. I do."

Dudly inquired, "Jason, have you ever had a friend in your life that you didn't give your grandfather's money to or whom you didn't buy things for?"

Jason answered, "Well, there was Emily."

Dudly appeared reverent as he asked, "Are you referring to the late daughter of your fiancée?"

Jason answered, "Yes."

Dudly glanced at me and at Alexia seated at the counsel table. "With all due respect, I believe that would be classified as more of a family relationship."

Dudly shifted like a chameleon. "So, Jason, back to my question. Have you ever had a friend in your life that you didn't give your grandfather's money to or whom you didn't buy things for?"

Jason seemed to think back into his past, then he shook his

head and said, "No, thanks to my grandfather I always had a lot of money, so I always bought things and helped my friends out."

"And that's the same way you met Brian?" Dudly asked.

Jason replied, "Well, I guess so."

Dudly shot back, "How many of these friends have you seen and how many have contacted you since all of your grandfather's assets were frozen?"

Jason looked down at the floor and said, "Well, not really any."

Dudly appeared triumphant and declared, "Witness dismissed. Your Honor, anyone would act like a friend as long as someone was giving them money, paying their expenses, and buying them things. This is not the definition of a friend nor does it meet the criteria set forth in the last will and testament of Red Stevens."

Hamilton blurted out, "Your Honor, we object to counsel's assertion that having money or sharing money necessarily eliminates the elements of a true and lasting friendship. You can't buy a friend with money, nor can you lose their friendship simply because you've shared what you have."

I was torn. Both Hamilton and Dudly had scored significant points. The evidence was not overwhelming as it had been in The Gift of Work and The Gift of Money.

I took a deep breath stalling for time, and then I remembered old Judge Eldridge's words: *Never make any decision before you have to.*

I smiled and mentally thanked my mentor for the thousandth time and spoke: "At this time, the court does not find evidence to conclusively support the fact that Jason Stevens has mastered The Gift of Friends."

A cacophony of shouts, whistles, and cheers rose from the

assorted Stevens clan arrayed behind Dudly. I pounded my gavel mercilessly and glared at them until the silence of a tomb descended.

I growled, "Counselor, inform your clients that we will have order in this court. This is not a football game or even a polo match."

I let the silence draw out before I continued. "On the other hand, the court finds no conclusive evidence to demonstrate that the friendships formed by Jason Stevens are not legitimate; therefore, the court will reserve judgment and hope the evidence will be more clear in thirty days when Mr. Stevens can demonstrate that he has the ability to not only make friends but pass along The Gift of Friends to others.

"This court is adjourned."

In my chambers, I gazed at the many photos on the wall. There were pictures from law school and a number of photos with associates and colleagues. I wondered how many, if any, of these people would meet the courtroom criteria of a friend. I was hoping for clarity and inspiration as I slid the DVD labeled *The Gift of Friends* into the player.

Red Stevens appeared as if he had always been there and always would be. He spoke. "*Friend* is a word that is thrown around far too easily by people who don't know the meaning of it. Today, people call everyone they know their friend. Young man, you're lucky if you live as long as I have and can count your real friends on the fingers of both hands.

"I am now going to share a story with you, Jason, that I promised I would never tell as long as I lived. Since you are watching this after my death, and in the presence of the one whom I promised, I feel comfortable sharing it. As you know, I lived past my seventy-fifth birthday and enjoyed what to most people was a long and healthy life. But this was not always a sure thing.

"I remember when I had just turned thirty-eight years old and was hospitalized with an extreme fever. The doctors weren't sure what was wrong with me, so they brought in every specialist from across the country. Finally, I was diagnosed as having a rare kidney disease, which was incurable. The only hope they gave me was a new procedure called a kidney transplant.

"You've got to realize that this was unheard of at that time, and donors were not readily available as they are today. I called Mr. Hamilton, who has always acted as my attorney, and told him we would need to start a nationwide search to find a kidney. I was very frightened because the specialist had told me that without the transplant I might not have more than a few weeks. You can imagine my relief when Mr. Hamilton called me two days later and told me he had located a kidney on the East Coast.

"Well, as I'm sure you can guess, the operation was a success and gave me back almost half of my adult life. What I'm sure you couldn't guess, and what no one has known until now, is that the kidney that Mr. Hamilton found was his own.

"There's only one way in the world to explain something like that, and it's called friendship."

I sat back in my familiar leather chair and tried to catch my breath. I thought about the emotions involved with giving someone one of my kidneys, and I further thought about having a friend at a level so deep that they would give up their kidney for me.

The image haunted me. I was questioning whether I had

anyone like that in my life when the phone on my desk rang. I had told the switchboard to hold all my calls, so I knew who it was. As I picked up the phone and said, "Hello, Marie," I knew beyond a shadow of a doubt that I had someone like that in my life and she, in turn, had me. I would continue thinking about The Gift of Friends and how it related to my life, but I knew that I first and foremost would always be grateful for the fact that I had found my best friend and asked her to marry me.

———

The month dragged by, but eventually I found myself back in court dealing with *The Case*.

As I called the court to order, I just stared at Theodore J. Hamilton. I couldn't get the story Red Stevens had told out of my mind. I had always considered Theodore J. Hamilton an incomparable practitioner of the law. Now I knew him to have been an incomparable friend. He stared back at me, and somehow I was sure that he knew that I was aware of his Gift of Friendship with Red Stevens. I nodded at him in greeting, and he smiled and actually winked at me.

I gestured for him to proceed. Jason took his now-familiar place on the witness stand, and Theodore J. Hamilton asked, "Jason, during the last month, have you had an opportunity to explore and demonstrate your ability not only to understand friendship but to impart that gift to others?"

Jason nodded, and Hamilton said, "Please share your experience with us."

Jason cleared his throat and started, "When I left here last month, I wasn't sure what to do since Mr. Dudly doesn't seem to count people who know you have money as friends. With all of the TV reports and everything because of this trial, everybody knows me.

"Then I remembered a young man I met last year named David Reese. David is a blind guy I met while learning about The Gift of Laughter. I heard that David was teaching over at the school for the blind across town. I called him, and he told me he was teaching sort of an introduction class for newly blinded people or those just entering the school. I told David I was looking for a group of people to discuss The Gift of Friends with, and David thought this would be a really good part of his class."

Jason looked toward Hamilton for approval, but Hamilton was reviewing notes. Miss Hastings, seated next to Hamilton, smiled at Jason angelically, and Jason continued confidently.

"Well, I thought that since all the people would be blind, they wouldn't have seen me on TV and wouldn't know who I was or that I might be rich. So I went to the class and, after David introduced me, I told about twenty-five blind people that I couldn't imagine having to make the adjustment they were all making and I really respected their efforts. I also told them that I thought if I were going through something like they were, that I would want and need my friends around me.

"They all agreed, but some of them shared that after becoming blind they had lost a lot of their friends. They felt it was probably because people were uncomfortable and just didn't know how to react to them. We went around the room and talked about what we needed from friends and what we each thought we had to offer. I connected with several people that day who I hope will be my friends in the future.

"One of the things we all discovered was that in order to have a friend, you have to be a friend. I was struggling to think of how these people could reach out and be a friend to others. Then I remembered the senior citizens' center I had driven past on my way to the school for the blind. I told them that there must be hundreds of people there who would really appreciate and welcome a telephone call. Some of these calls would just be a pleasant encouragement, while others might blossom into friendship."

Jason reached into his inside jacket pocket and withdrew a folded sheaf of papers. He looked up at me questioningly as he continued.

"Your Honor, I'm not sure who to give this to, but this is a list of all the people who are making regular phone calls to the elderly and a number of letters from the elderly people describing how making new friends has made their lives better."

I followed the direction of Jason's gaze and observed Miss Hastings with tears in her eyes smiling back at Jason.

Hamilton quipped, "I believe the young man has spoken for himself."

Jason was glancing between me and the court reporter, holding out the bundle of papers questioningly.

Dudly interceded, "I'll take that, and I do have a few questions."

Dudly rifled through the pages quickly and said, "So, Jason, let me get this straight. In order to find friends, you went to a school for blind people and a nursing home. Wouldn't you agree these are not traditional places to find friends?"

Jason shrugged and answered, "I don't know. I just went to the school for the blind so that I could meet people who hadn't seen my picture on TV or in the papers. I thought I could stay anonymous."

Dudly smirked and inquired, "Well, did you stay anonymous, or did you or your friend David let all these people know that you stand to gain control of several billion dollars if you somehow deprive my clients of their inheritance?"

I glanced over, anticipating Hamilton's objection, but he just smiled and waved his hand dismissively.

Jason responded, "Well, I didn't tell them who I was, but they kind of found out."

Dudly pressed the issue. "And how, pray tell, did this breach of security involving your identity occur?"

Jason chuckled and replied, "Well, it was after the class and the times we spent together coordinating the calls with the senior citizens when David and several students at the school for the blind actually laughed at me quite a bit and told me how ridiculous I was to think they wouldn't recognize my voice from the TV and radio. They all knew me instantly, and they asked about the case."

Dudly continued down this path, asking, "Just exactly what did they ask about the case?"

Jason shook his head and mumbled, "Oh, nothing really specific."

Dudly drew himself to his full height and demanded, "Young man, you are under oath. What specifically did they ask you about these proceedings?"

Jason responded innocently, "They wanted to know if you really worked for a firm named Dudly, Cheetham, and Leech."

Laughter could be heard throughout the courtroom as I tapped my gavel for quiet.

Dudly recovered some of his dignity and changed course. "Mr.

THE LIFE OF FRIENDS

Stevens, exactly what formula or recipe do you feel you followed at the school for the blind or the nursing home that could indicate to this court that you have the ability to find or create friendships?"

Jason glanced up at me then back at Mr. Dudly, answering, "I couldn't guarantee anybody anything. Friendship and friends are gifts we receive. The only thing we can do is plant the seeds and help other people plant them; and occasionally when we're really fortunate, a friendship will grow and blossom and provide seeds for more friendships in the future."

Dudly just stared at Jason dumbfounded.

Finally I broke the silence, inquiring of Dudly, "Counselor, any further questions?"

Dudly shook his head and returned to his counsel table. I smiled at Jason and told him that would be all.

I stared at Mr. Hamilton as I ruled. "I believe we've all learned something about friendship in this place today. The court wishes to thank Jason Stevens for his lesson and commend him on not only being a friend but helping others become friends as well. I would encourage everyone here to think on these things.

"This court is adjourned until 10:00 a.m. Monday."

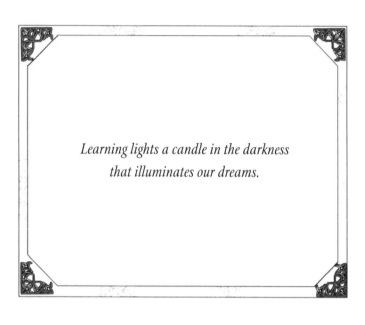

Learning lights a candle in the darkness
that illuminates our dreams.

Six

THE LIFE OF LEARNING

It was a blessed weekend. Some weekends are merely accustomed parentheses at the end of a work week. Other weekends are a needed prescription for an overburdened soul.

Marie informed me Friday night as we were dining at one of our favorite restaurants that she had scheduled some family activities for us over the weekend. The term *family activities* could otherwise be loosely translated into chores. My family activities, among other things, were to involve raking leaves, cleaning out guttering, and trying to rearrange the garage so it might hold two cars this winter instead of one. I was about to lodge a complaint as I considered all of that work with the only prize being to get one additional car in the garage when I remembered that the additional car in the garage this winter would be mine.

Marie and I had a delightful dinner remembering good times past and planning trips and holiday celebrations in the future. I am always amazed and thankful that after knowing this person over fifty years, we have yet to run out of things to talk about. In fact, the years—instead of exhausting the possibilities between us—have opened vistas we can still explore together.

I think we both tried to avoid it as long as possible, but like an elephant in the living room, it was simply unavoidable, and eventually we settled on the topic of *The Case*. Marie knows that I am opposed to discussing ongoing cases other than the aspects of the trial that may have been introduced into the media. The media coverage of the Red Stevens' contested will case had been so thorough I felt comfortable in discussing any and all matters surrounding *The Case*.

Marie asked, "Why do you think the family can't just be satisfied with hundreds of millions? Why do they have to go after the billions of dollars Jason was to manage through the charitable trust?"

I thought for a minute and then offered a possible explanation. "After seeing thousands of people come and go through my courtroom, fighting over money, property, and all manner of personal possessions, it has come to my attention that there is a disease rampant among humans. The disease is called *more*. It is a veritable epidemic.

"People who have nothing want something. People who have something want a lot. People who have a lot want everything. And people who have everything want more. It just never ends. Otherwise contented and well-adjusted people can learn that someone else is receiving something, and all of a sudden what they had is no longer enough. They want still more."

Marie frowned and shook her head. She commented, "It's too bad those kinds of people can't travel abroad as you and I have and see the abject poverty in which most of the world is living."

I nodded, thinking about some of the heart-wrenching sights of poverty I had seen as I spoke. "That would seem to be logical; however, some of the wealthiest people I have ever known will step over a wounded homeless person in the gutter as they rush to a meeting to try to make their next million.

"There is a balance that must be achieved. The drive to be successful is what has made our country great. Scientific breakthroughs and medical advances are a part of this ongoing effort and striving. On the other hand, people must come to understand how, in a global sense, we are all wealthy beyond imagination."

Marie sipped her coffee and said, "It's sad, because you are in a roomful of Stevens' family members, all of whom have enough wealth for a hundred lifetimes. But their greed has put them in a position where someone is going to walk away with absolutely nothing."

I chuckled as I thought about that eventuality.

"These are people who have never learned how to make it without money. Being poor is a skill that must be learned and cultivated."

Marie laughed and said, "Your Honor, I remember those days very well. Law school wasn't cheap, and we both learned how to sleep on the floor and eat whatever was on sale during double coupon day. I wouldn't want to go back to that."

I responded, "I agree, but some of our best times were then, and we both know if we had to we could survive on next to nothing. The Stevens family simply doesn't know what they don't know. There's a whole world out there that they've never been exposed to."

Dessert arrived, which called for lighter, more pleasant table conversation. We settled into talk of grandchildren and gardening.

As we were walking out of the restaurant arm-in-arm, I commented, "I needed that."

"The food was good," Marie said.

I stopped and looked deeply into those familiar and still-fascinating eyes and said, "I don't mean the food."

As I climbed up to the bench and settled into my chair, I noticed that I was quite sore in my lower back. A remnant, no doubt, of the several hours of raking leaves, otherwise known as *family activities*.

I tapped my gavel for order, nodded a greeting to the overflowing courtroom, and announced, "Today we will take up the matter of The Gift of Learning. I want to remind everyone of the gravity of this case and the fact that this is an ongoing matter that, unlike most estate cases, will not be resolved in a day or two. This case will be heard periodically over an entire year and holds serious consequences for the parties involved.

"If the Stevens family, represented by Mr. Dudly ..." I paused, glanced toward Dudly, and motioned to that side of the courtroom, "... is successful in overturning the Red Stevens' will and attached Ultimate Gift provisions, they will divide among themselves several billion dollars currently frozen in the Red Stevens' Charitable Trust.

"On the other hand ..." I looked toward Mr. Hamilton, Jason, his fiancée Alexia, Hamilton's able assistant Miss Hastings, and the ever-present but silent Jeffrey Watkins and announced, "... on the other hand, if Mr. Jason Stevens, represented by Theodore J. Hamilton, is successful in defending the last will of Red Stevens, including The Ultimate Gift provisions, the charitable trust will remain in place and be under the sole direction of Jason Stevens; and the resources inherited by the Stevens family members will be forfeited as they have contested the will, and those resources will be added to the Red Stevens' Charitable Trust.

"Although this case is very unorthodox and I have granted extreme latitude in the display and demonstration of evidence, I caution counsel and all those present that this is, indeed, a most serious court proceeding, and I will expect everyone to act accordingly."

I gazed judicially about my courtroom and then glanced toward Hamilton.

"Mr. Hamilton, I call on you and your client to make your case before this court that Jason Stevens has, in fact, lived up to the provisions of The Ultimate Gift as outlined by Red Stevens with respect to The Gift of Learning."

Theodore J. Hamilton, following my admonition to treat this matter as a formal court proceeding, rose in a dignified manner and intoned, "Your Honor, we call Jason Stevens to the stand."

Jason rose from his chair, moved around the counsel table, and took his place in the witness box.

I reminded everyone that Jason Stevens had already been

sworn in this matter, and he was still under oath with regard to his testimony in these proceedings.

Hamilton began. "Jason, as a part of your grandfather's Gift of Learning, you made a trip to South America."

Jason nodded affirmatively, and Hamilton encouraged him. "Would you tell us about your experiences there?"

Jason replied, "I traveled to a rather remote village where my grandfather had established a library for the people of the region. I worked on reorganizing and categorizing books in the library."

Hamilton inquired, "What did you discover about The Gift of Learning while performing your duties in the library?"

Jason paused to reflect before continuing. "First, I learned that the people of the region have a hunger for learning. They don't have access to schools, books, libraries, and computers like we do. I was surprised when I first got to the library to learn that most of the books were gone. The librarian told me that the majority of the books were always checked out and were distributed among even more remote villages encompassing an area of many miles."

Hamilton directed the testimony by asking, "Isn't it true that you were actually kidnapped during your time in South America and imprisoned by a group of drug lords?"

Jason recounted, "Yes. It was the most frightening experience of my life. I fully expected to be killed at any time."

Hamilton inquired, "Did you acquire any knowledge about The Gift of Learning during your imprisonment?"

Jason nodded and spoke, "While I was in my prison cell, occasionally pages of a book would be passed to me by other prisoners. They were in Spanish, which took me a long time to decipher. I came to treasure the moments when these pages would appear, as they seemed to be my lifeline to the outside world and any hope of being free again. I will never forget the value of even one page of a book."

Hamilton nodded as if thoroughly satisfied and announced, "That will be all."

Theodore J. Hamilton returned to his accustomed spot at the end of the counsel table. I looked across the aisle and gestured at Mr. Dudly.

He spoke. "Yes, Your Honor, we have several lines of inquiry regarding this so-called learning experience or field trip into the jungle that Jason Stevens took last year."

I looked at Hamilton anticipating an objection, but he just smiled at me and shook his head as if it didn't really matter.

Dudly continued, "Mr. Stevens, isn't it true that you flunked out of or were otherwise expelled for disciplinary reasons from ..." Dudly referred to a file folder and continued. "... at least nine different prep schools before you allegedly graduated from high school?"

Jason shrugged and replied, "I don't know the exact number, but that's probably about right."

"Mr. Stevens," Dudly continued, "it appears to me that you had the benefit of attending some of the finest private schools in the United States. How is it that with all of these advantages you either failed to perform even minimally or, in many cases, were removed for disciplinary reasons?"

Jason cleared his throat and spoke. "Well, I guess you could say I wasn't very motivated when I was a school-aged kid."

Dudly glared at Jason, replying, "I think that would be a gross understatement, but let us go on. The story seems to be even more fascinating."

Dudly paced back and forth. His momentum was building.

"You apparently somehow, thanks to the generous contributions of your grandfather, got into several elite universities and somehow walked away with a sketchy and dubious degree that seems to correspond with a sizable gift from your family to the endowment of that institution. But, once again, you apparently did not attend class and, when you did show up, you failed to perform at a level that achieved anything other than failing grades."

He stared at Jason and inquired, "Is that about right?"

Jason nodded reluctantly and admitted, "Yes."

Dudly continued pacing back and forth and spoke. "Now let us focus our attention on this little trip to South America. Mr. Stevens, did you have any knowledge of the culture, customs, or even the language of the people served by the Red Stevens' Library in South America?"

Jason shook his head and stated, "No. I had never heard of the place. I didn't know anything about it, and I couldn't speak the language."

"So," Dudly continued, "we are to understand that you worked in a library and somehow organized books that were written in a language you could not even read."

Jason nodded his head and said, "Yes."

Dudly built to a crescendo. "We will not even address your so-called kidnapping and confinement relating to any scraps of paper you may have received. It would be absurd to put any of that activity in the context of The Gift of Learning."

Hamilton announced automatically, "Your Honor, we object.

If counsel is not going to address the matter, please ask him to save his commentary for someone who might care."

I glanced at Mr. Dudly and said, "Objection sustained. Mr. Dudly, please confine your cross-examination to questions for this witness."

Dudly waved dismissively and stated, "Your Honor, we have no further questions for this witness as nothing he has ever done or said here today could lend itself even slightly toward demonstrating that he understands The Gift of Learning, much less is he equipped and prepared to pass this learning on to others."

Dudly took his seat at the counsel table across the aisle from Mr. Hamilton. Both lawyers and everyone in the courtroom looked toward me with great anticipation. I felt the tension building.

Old Judge Eldridge's words came back to me once again. *Never make any decision before you have to.*

My gaze rose to the giant ornate clock on the back wall of the courtroom.

I spoke. "As it is approaching midday, court will stand in recess until 2:00 p.m."

I struck my gavel once and retreated to the sanity of my chambers.

As Red Stevens' countenance appeared on the video screen, I hoped he would have some answers for me about The Gift of Learning.

"As you know, I never had the benefit of a formal education, and I realize that you have some kind of degree from that high-toned college we sent you to that is little more than a playground for the idle rich.

"Now, before you get your feelings all hurt, I want you to realize that I respect universities as well as any type of formal education. It just wasn't a part of my life. What was a part of my life was a constant curiosity and desire to learn everything I could about the people and world around me. I wasn't able to go to school very long after I learned to read, but the ability to read, think, and observe made me a relatively well-educated man.

"But learning is a process. You can't simply sit in a classroom and someday walk offstage with a sheepskin and call yourself educated. I believe the reason a graduation ceremony is called a *commencement* is because the process of learning begins—commences—at that point. The schooling that went before simply provided the tools and the framework for the real lessons to come.

"In the final analysis, Jason, life—when lived on your own terms—is the ultimate teacher. My wealth and success have robbed you of that, and this is my best effort to repair the damage."

————

At 2:00 p.m. sharp, I reentered the courtroom and couldn't help but notice the Stevens clan eagerly assembled in their customary seats. There appeared to be great anticipation on that side of the aisle. Dudly was beaming.

I pounded my gavel and declared, "Court is back in session. With respect to the ruling on The Gift of Learning, I find that Mr.

Dudly is correct in that Jason Stevens has never demonstrated even an average aptitude for school or the formal pursuit of learning."

A cheer and smattering of applause could be heard from the Stevens family. I glared at them until silence resumed.

"However ..." A corresponding moan could be heard from Dudly's side of the courtroom. "... Howard 'Red' Stevens had some nontraditional and informal ideas regarding The Gift of Learning. Red Stevens felt that education was a lifelong process, not a brief activity or accomplishment; therefore, it is the finding of this court that Jason Stevens has demonstrated that he understands The Gift of Learning. During the next thirty days, he will be given an opportunity to demonstrate that he can impact others with this Gift of Learning received from his grandfather.

"This court stands adjourned. This matter will be taken up again in thirty days."

I rapped my gavel.

It was thirty days later. Jason Stevens was, once again, in the witness box as Theodore J. Hamilton approached.

"Jason, over the past month, have you had the opportunity to pass along The Gift of Learning shared with you by your grandfather?"

Jason nodded and said, "Yes," as Hamilton motioned him to continue. "I was struggling to decide how my grandfather would pass on The Gift of Learning. I decided to take a walk in the Howard 'Red' Stevens Urban Park. Sometimes I feel closer to him there."

Jason looked timidly toward Mr. Watkins seated next to Miss Hastings at the counsel table. They both nodded encouragingly as Jason continued.

"While I was walking through the park, I noticed a group of ten- or twelve-year-old boys gathered there. This struck me as strange as it was a school day. I went over and talked to them and asked why they weren't in school. They shared with me that they didn't care about school, and you couldn't learn anything important in that school anyway.

"I asked what school they went to and found out the name of their teacher. I went to the school and waited for class to be out and then went in to meet their teacher."

Jason loosened his tie slightly and sat back in the witness chair. He glanced up at me briefly and went on.

"It's a really rundown inner-city school. It looks like they spend more money on armed guards than they do on teaching the kids. The teacher I met was a young guy my age named Tom. Tom has spent his whole life preparing to be a teacher, and he is totally dedicated to these kids; but Tom told me most of their parents aren't involved, and the kids just don't see anything in his lessons relevant to the world they know.

"I asked what subjects these kids were studying. Tom told me they were learning fractions, geometry, beginning economics, and they all had to prepare a science fair project. I worked it out with Tom for me to create a supplemental Saturday School in the inner-city park every week."

Mr. Hamilton nodded as if in approval of the progress that Jason had made and inquired, "How has your Saturday School been going?"

Jason smiled with pride and said, "Well, we've had class for four weeks. In order to get into my Saturday School, you have to have a library card and a note from the teacher that you have been in class every day the previous week. We invited kids from surrounding schools and older kids in the day care run by the single moms' co-op."

Jason paused to organize his thoughts and then discreetly counted off the four weeks' activities on his fingers as he spoke. "The first week, I got all the kids to come because I announced that the shortstop for the area Major League baseball team would be at the Saturday School that first week. He talked about batting averages, and he and Tom worked together so kids began to understand and be excited about learning percentages and fractions. He gave all the kids signed baseball cards.

"The second week, we met at the basketball court in the park, and the starting forward for the NBA franchise showed up to help us demonstrate geometry. He made shots from all angles of the court using the backboard to demonstrate the various angles and how they changed, depending on where he was shooting from.

"The third week, we had a lesson in economics. A self-made millionaire businessman, who had attended their school thirty years ago, showed up in a limo and explained why it was important to understand business and finance. The kids all got to ride in the limo, and Tom said they are really interested in beginning economics now.

"Last week, I had a NASCAR driver come to the park and bring his race car. He told the kids and demonstrated how a high-performance engine works. He explained that you can't be a race-car driver or much of anything else unless you understand basic science. The kids got energized and excited about their science fair projects, and things are getting a lot better at the school."

I looked at Mr. Hamilton and inquired, "Any further questions, counselor?"

Hamilton grinned and replied, "Your Honor, I believe that's more than enough."

Dudly rose and barked, "Your Honor, a number of questions regarding this whole situation are begging to be asked."

I sighed and responded, "Please ask your questions."

Dudly was undaunted as he approached Jason.

"Mr. Stevens, do you have a teaching certificate from this state or any jurisdiction?"

Jason shook his head, appearing bewildered and replied, "No."

"Does your baseball player, basketball player, businessman, or race-car driver have teaching certificates or credentials that this court might recognize?"

Jason shrugged and said, "I don't know, but I doubt it."

Dudly continued. "Does this teacher named Tom you refer to have permission from the school board to conduct official sanctioned classes in this so-called urban park?"

Jason shrugged again and responded, "I'm not sure. It is just a bunch of kids who need a new way to learn in order to get excited about school, combined with a few high-profile individuals who are willing to volunteer their time to help."

Dudly swirled about grandly as if addressing everyone seated in the courtroom. "Well, I certainly don't find anything educational or approaching The Gift of Learning in that."

"Well, I do," I ruled. "Counselor, do you have any further questions in this matter?"

Dudly appeared deflated and shook his head in defeat.

I concluded, "Then this matter is resolved. This court will be in session at 10:00 a.m. to take up The Gift of Problems."

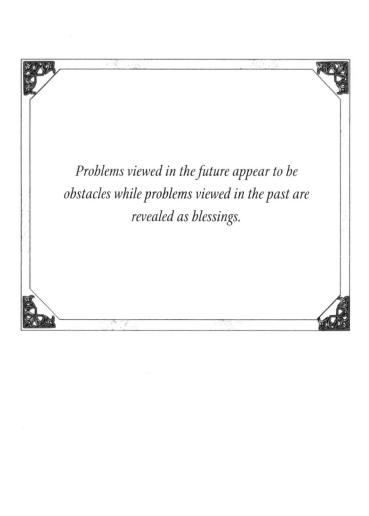

Problems viewed in the future appear to be obstacles while problems viewed in the past are revealed as blessings.

$EVEN

THE LIFE OF PROBLEMS

If my chambers in the court building, with the exception of my own leather chair, were designed by people to impress other people, my study at home was designed by me to impress no one other than me. The photos displayed are for the sole purpose of helping me to recall times, places, and people who matter only to me. While the array of pictures might not impress anyone else, they are, without a doubt, the photographic milestones of my life.

My desk is huge, but unlike the one in the court building, it is functional. Every inch of the surface is covered with what appears to be chaotic debris; but, in reality, I know where everything is and can put my fingers on it whenever I choose. The fact that the disorganization would baffle anyone else is somehow comforting to me.

There are a number of well-worn law books that share shelf space with books on everything from golf to fishing and novels ranging from westerns to science fiction. My Labrador retriever,

Rex, has found his own familiar and comfortable spot on the ancient rug in front of the fireplace. Like me, he doesn't ask for anything during his time in the study other than to be left alone and to have everything left permanently as it is.

I was breaking one of my study's unwritten rules as I was thinking about the day in court; however, since it's one of my rules and since it's my study where I have sole and absolute jurisdiction, I can suspend or amend rules whenever I wish.

Rex and I were preparing to watch a football game on the large television nearby. It wasn't just any football game, but the hometown team was playing the evil instate rival. I realize there are many sections of the United States that do not even have a professional football team, but I still feel one of the great developments in the game was when they put two pro teams in the same state. I had the hometown jersey on and my refreshments arrayed before me.

The aforementioned jersey has been the subject of several debates with my beloved Marie, as the jersey is now older than the oldest player currently in the League. Approximately a decade ago, Marie informed me that my football jersey should be donated to a charity resale shop. In recent debates, she has downgraded its proposed disposal to inclusion in our family rag bag for washing the cars.

Since the jersey is worn only in my study where I have supreme jurisdiction, she has relented but has laid down a ruling pertaining to her jurisdiction, which includes everywhere outside of my study. Marie's ruling states that the football jersey in question can never be worn outside of the study, particularly if we're going anywhere or having people come over.

Since I didn't want to go anywhere or see anyone, the football jersey was an ideal wardrobe selection. I had asked Rex the Wonder Dog if he disagreed. Hearing no comments to the contrary, I knew we were in one accord.

I was tuned in to the appropriate channel waiting for the ball game. Then just before the pre-game broadcast, the network went for a news update.

There she was, standing next to L. Myron Dudly. It was Sarah Stevens—Jason Stevens' mother and one of the litigants opposing him in the Red Stevens matter.

Sarah was asked, "Why would you oppose your own son in the court case?"

She smiled for the camera and spoke as if discussing a delightful dinner party or fashion accessory.

"Jason is a good boy. He's just confused. This is not really an argument. We're just clearing up some of those nasty, nagging legal things."

The reporter continued, "Don't you feel Jason should be allowed to give away your father-in-law's money as Red Stevens intended through the charitable trust?"

Sarah giggled and offered her comments. "Well, charity's fine, but this is money that my father-in-law worked for, and it should go to his children. Besides, we do a lot for charity."

"How much do you do for charity?" the reporter fired at her.

Sarah seemed perplexed. Dudly stammered as if to stop Sarah, but Sarah answered, "Well, I know I help a lot of charities. Just last week, I donated a whole bag of clothing, and we always buy a table for the opera, ball, and the ballet, and ... well, you know. All the right things."

The reporter asked, "Sarah, are you in communication with your son, Jason?"

Sarah smiled and said, "Well, we don't talk any less now than we always have."

As the reporter was beginning to thank Sarah Stevens and throw it back to the anchor, Dudly interrupted authoritatively, "I believe my client has answered all the questions she needs to. We will have no further comment on this matter."

The reporter appeared bewildered as the screen faded to black and the football game came on.

I was totally distracted and reaching for the remote control to turn off the game when I noticed that Rex was focused on the TV in anticipation. Since I had promised him all week we would watch the game together, I tossed him a pretzel and kept my commitment.

———————

The next morning, as usual, I greeted the sunrise as it appeared through the window of my chambers. I located the DVD copy of the video Red Stevens had made for Jason labeled *The Gift of Problems*. I was thinking that the phrase "The Gift of Problems" seems to be ironic when Red Stevens began to speak.

"Jason, life is full of many contradictions. In fact, the longer you live, the more the reality of life will seem like one great paradox. But if you live long enough and search hard enough you will find a miraculous order to the confusion.

"All of the lessons I am trying to teach you as a part of The Ultimate Gift left through my will are generally learned as people go through their lives facing struggles and problems. Any challenge that does not defeat us ultimately strengthens us.

"One of the great errors in my life was sheltering so many people—including you—from life's problems. Out of a misguided sense of concern for your well-being, I actually took away your ability to handle life's problems by removing them from your environment.

"Unfortunately, human beings cannot live in a vacuum forever. A bird must struggle in order to emerge from the eggshell. A well-meaning person might crack open the egg, releasing the baby bird. This person might walk away feeling as though he has done the bird a wonderful service when, in fact, he has left the bird in a weakened condition and unable to deal with its environment. Instead of helping the bird, the person has, in fact, destroyed it. It is only a matter of time until something in the bird's environment attacks it, and the bird has no ability to deal with what otherwise would be a manageable problem.

"If we are not allowed to deal with small problems, we will be destroyed by slightly larger ones. When we come to understand this fact, we live our lives not avoiding problems but welcoming them as challenges that will strengthen us so that we can be victorious in the future."

I thought about the perspective of actually welcoming problems. I remembered many of the good things that had happened in my personal and professional life and had to admit they were each accompanied by a number of problems.

The appointed hour arrived. I donned my black judicial robes, made my way through the mahogany door, and mounted the three steps to my familiar perch above the courtroom. I settled in and asked everyone to be seated. I reviewed my case notes, removed my reading glasses, and gazed at the overflowing crowd.

The ensuing months of this case had not diminished the media frenzy nor the curiosity surrounding Red Stevens and his last will and testament.

I cleared my throat and began. "Today, we are beginning the fifth of twelve provisions outlined in the estate of Howard 'Red' Stevens. This hearing will focus on The Gift of Problems. I will call on counsel for Jason Stevens, Mr. Theodore J. Hamilton, to bring us up to date on how the provisions were handled in this matter."

Hamilton rose with amazing grace and agility for a gentleman well past eighty. He sensed my more formal demeanor with respect to this hearing and acted accordingly.

"Thank you, Your Honor. Once again, the matter before this court is to determine and verify that each tenet of the last will and testament of Howard 'Red' Stevens was carried out appropriately and the bequest awarded to Jason Stevens was, and is, in order."

Hamilton paused for effect, but Dudly jumped in. "Your Honor, counsel should understand after five monthly hearings that the purpose of this case is to scrutinize the absurd bequest in the form of a charitable trust given to Jason Stevens depriving the three children and other heirs who are direct descendants of Red Stevens of their rightful inheritance."

Hamilton laughed aloud and responded, "That may be your purpose in being here, Mr. Dud ..." The now-familiar coughing fit erupted. Hamilton regained control and continued. "... but my purpose here is quite different. I would ask opposing counsel to make his own case and allow me to make mine."

I was forced to intervene as if dealing with two squabbling children. "Counselors, I fully understand why you each are here and the positions of the parties you represent; therefore, if we can suspend the superfluous soliloquies I will ask Mr. Hamilton to make his case."

Hamilton motioned for Jason to take his place, and he began his questioning.

"Jason, do you recall the month you spent, under the direction of your grandfather's will, exploring The Gift of Problems?"

Jason responded solemnly, "Yes, sir. I do. I think I can safely say it was both the best and the worst time in my life."

"Can you explain that?" Hamilton inquired.

Jason glanced cautiously toward his fiancée, Alexia, seated next to Miss Hastings at the counsel table. Miss Hastings placed her hand atop Alexia's hand as Jason spoke.

"My grandfather said that I should go out and find people who were experiencing real problems in their lives, and I should learn the lessons that came with their problems."

Hamilton nodded in understanding and asked, "So what did you do?"

Jason was fighting emotion as he spoke. "I went for a walk to think about The Gift of Problems. I passed a park and noticed a young girl swinging, while her mother watched her with a somber look on her face. I went to meet them and found out that Emily, the daughter, had terminal cancer."

I couldn't help but notice a few tears on Alexia's face as Jason continued.

"I got to know Emily and her mother, Alexia ..." Jason pointed toward his fiancée. "... during the time Emily had left."

"Can you help us understand what you learned from little Emily during the last months of her life?"

Jason's voice broke and tears began to form as he remembered that time. "Emily got sicker and sicker, no matter what anyone did. I know it had to be painful and terrifying for a little kid like that. She never complained, and she taught me so many things through her problems and suffering.

"First, she taught me about joy—that no matter what the circumstance, people can be happy simply because they have decided to be happy people. Then she taught me about courage— that there's really nothing to be afraid of that is any worse than living a life full of fear. And, finally, she taught me how to love. I learned to love her as an unforgettable and special part of my life. And she taught me how to love her mother, and she left us both with that special love. I hope to spend the rest of my life with Alexia, learning how to love and live out all of the lessons I learned from Emily and her problems."

Hamilton was emotional and touched Jason's hand, which lay atop the rail in front of him.

He said, "Thank you, son. That wasn't easy, but it was important."

Hamilton cleared his throat, looked at me, and said, "Your Honor, we will let that be enough for now."

Dudly rose to speak. He actually restored some of my faith in lawyers as he said, "Your Honor, we accept these provisions regarding this matter as stated."

I nodded with some new respect for Mr. Dudly and said, "Thank you, Mr. Dudly."

I wiped my eyes and stated, "Mr. Stevens has demonstrated to this court beyond a shadow of a doubt that he has fully experienced and learned The Gift of Problems. During the next thirty days, he will be given the opportunity to demonstrate that he has the ability to utilize the Red Stevens Charitable Trust to impart an understanding of The Gift of Problems to other people. This court is adjourned."

I rushed into my chambers and engaged in an emotional display that would not be becoming the dignity of a sitting judge, but it was the thing to do. I thought about a special little girl who, through her dying, taught me and everyone in the courtroom a lot about how we should be living.

A month later, we were all back in our places. Jason, under the direction of Theodore J. Hamilton, was recounting his recent activities with respect to The Gift of Problems.

"Alexia and I decided that we had to help other people who were going through what we went through." Jason smiled at Alexia, and she returned the gesture. He pressed on. "We decided that one of the biggest problems that anyone could ever face would be a parent losing a child. Alexia and I felt compelled to help these people as I believe they can only be helped by someone who has faced that same tragedy.

"A book or a lecture or some well-meaning person who hasn't been there isn't going to cut it. You never really get past it or through it, but we believe that with the help of someone that has gone ahead of you, you can learn to live with it and actually grow as a result of it."

Hamilton nodded in agreement and understanding.

Jason continued. "Alexia and I went around to hospitals, clergy, and nursing homes and let them know that if and when they encountered parents experiencing the tragedy of losing a child, we would welcome the opportunity to just talk with them and share our experiences. In the last month, we have met with seven families who have lost or are losing a child. Some of them we've met with more than once. It's probably the hardest thing I've ever done, but I think it may be the best thing I'll ever do."

Hamilton nodded with approval at Jason. He turned to me and said, "Your Honor, that will be all."

I motioned toward Mr. Dudly inquiring, "Counselor, have you anything to add to the proceedings?"

Dudly spoke from his seat behind the counsel table. "We have no questions or arguments to put before the court."

L. Myron Dudly, his legal team, and even the Stevens family situated in the first few rows behind them all seemed to be moved. No one in the courtroom that day, including me, could escape the emotional impact and the life-altering message left by a little girl named Emily.

I tapped my gavel and ruled. "This matter is resolved by consent of counsel and ruling of the court. Tomorrow morning at 10:00 a.m., we will take up the matter of The Gift of Family."

Some families are formed by birth, others by legal documents, and still others are formed through love.

EIGHT

THE LIFE OF FAMILY

That next morning in my chambers, I prepared myself for what I knew would be a hotly contested issue surrounding The Gift of Family. Mr. Dudly and his team had wisely avoided any futile conflicts regarding The Gift of Problems, but I knew they would put on the pressure this day in the courtroom.

I kept my mind open and free from prejudice as any judge should do, but—at the same time—I allowed my thoughts to wander through the possibilities and the potential arguments I might hear.

The Stevens family was unique in many ways and dysfunctional in many other ways. Their money, power, influence, and occasional celebrity status had given them many advantages along with many disadvantages.

I couldn't help but think about my own family and the relatively simple life we have led. We had been forced to do without a lot of things that are available to rich and famous people, but we had experienced a depth of commitment and love that we would not trade for all the riches and fame the world has ever known.

I was so deep in thought that the time just escaped me. I said, "Come in," in response to a tap on my door, and Jim, my bailiff, stuck his head in and said, "Your Honor, everyone's ready whenever you are."

I glanced up at the clock as I was reaching for my robes. The official day in court was already two minutes old as I settled into my seat and gaveled the proceedings to order.

"Today, we are going to consider The Gift of Family. As this entire case is between family members, and related to family wealth, I anticipate that emotions may run high throughout these proceedings. As always, I want to caution counsel, clients, and everyone in the gallery that this is an official court proceeding that will be carried out with the order and respect it deserves. The court calls on Theodore J. Hamilton to address this matter."

Hamilton made his way around the counsel table and approached Jason who was already settling into the chair in the witness box.

Hamilton began. "Jason, can you share with us what you learned as a result of the lesson your grandfather, Red Stevens, gave to you through The Gift of Family?"

Jason nodded and began. "I went to the Red Stevens Boys' Home in Maine and spent an entire month working with a group of boys. Some of them had families that were not a part of their lives. Others had no family at all.

"It took me a while to learn that these kids at the Boys' Home had formed their own family. They worked together, played together, and encouraged one another in amazing ways. They taught me that a family is not always the traditional storybook family that we all wished we had, but sometimes a family is wherever you can find it."

Hamilton nodded as if satisfied, waved toward Dudly, and said, "Your witness."

L. Myron Dudly turned into a ferocious shark sensing blood in the water. He, along with his legal team and the Stevens family, knew this was one of the so-called hurdles where they had a good chance to prevail. This emotion was fueled by the fact that, if they could overturn just one of Jason's gifts that were a part of The Ultimate Gift in Red Stevens' will, they would divide several billion dollars among them. On the other hand, the fear of knowing that if they were defeated they would lose everything clung to them like a living thing.

Dudly attacked. "Mr. Stevens, you are before the court today apparently expecting us to believe that you understand The Gift of Family and are in a position to help others with this gift."

Jason nodded and simply replied, "Yes, sir."

Dudly continued. "It would be hard to think of anyone less qualified to speak to The Gift of Family than you."

"Your Honor," Hamilton thundered, "if counsel has a question, please encourage him to ask it or sit down."

I glared at Dudly, ruling, "Sustained. Mr. Dudly, do you have questions for this witness?"

Dudly bore in. "Mr. Stevens, you have testified before this court that you were so disconnected and so ashamed of Red Stevens that you would not even recognize the fact and admit that he was your grandfather."

Jason nodded feebly and almost whispered, "That's true."

Dudly had the grin of a shark sensing victory. "Mr. Stevens, your own family ..." Dudly motioned toward his side of the courtroom, "... has come together in this matter in opposition to you. They have had to mount a legal case for the sole purpose of protecting family assets that should rightfully be inherited by the direct descendants of Howard 'Red' Stevens. Don't you feel like you're tearing apart your family instead of displaying any understanding of The Gift of Family?"

Jason sighed and glanced toward Hamilton. He croaked, "I don't know how to answer that."

Dudly slapped his hands together and said, "I'm sure you don't know how to answer that. I wouldn't either."

Dudly paced back and forth, framing his next question. "Now, can you tell us how—even though you have no real relationship with your family—you became proficient in understanding the importance of families by simply spending a few weeks at some sort of boys' camp?"

Jason blurted out, "It's a Boys' Home."

Dudly mocked him as he bowed slightly and intoned, "Please excuse me. We will call it a Boys' Home."

Jason appeared to gain some momentum, stating, "I learned a lot of things there that would be hard to learn from people who have a good family life. I think it's difficult to know how important something is until it's not there. Without some of the lessons I learned from my grandfather and through the Boys' Home in The Gift of Family, I could not have made the beginning of a family with Alexia and Emily. I think when you get right down to it, the value of a family can only be judged by the people in the family."

Dudly rubbed his hands together and concluded, "Well, young man, in this case someone is going to have to judge you with respect to family, and I am imploring this court to rule on behalf of the Stevens family as the rightful heirs and natural family of their beloved patriarch, Howard 'Red' Stevens."

This matter was far from clear-cut, and I wanted to get some time and distance from the arguments before I made a decision. My head and the law I cherish so much were leaning one way. My heart and emotions were leaning the other way. I rapped my gavel and announced, "This court is in recess for lunch. We will resume these proceedings at 2:00 p.m."

I made my way into my chambers, threw off my judicial robes, and grabbed the DVD marked *The Gift of Family*. As I slid it into the player, I hoped and prayed that Red Stevens' message would somehow give me clarity and direction.

Red spoke to Jason. "Now, Jason, I realize that our family is about as messed up as a family can be, and I accept my full share of responsibility for that. However, the best or worst family situation can teach us a lesson. We either learn what we want or, sadly, we learn what we don't want in life from our families. Out of all the young men in the world, I have selected you. I have asked Mr. Hamilton to undertake this monumental task on my behalf for you. It's hard to understand why that means something, but I want you to know that it does.

"Families give us our roots, our heritage, and our past. They also give us the springboard to our future. Nothing in this world is stronger than the bond that can be formed by a family. That is a bond of pure love that will withstand any pressure as long as the love is kept in the forefront.

"It's important for you to realize that families come in all shapes and sizes. Some very blessed people are able to live their whole lives as part of the families they were born into. Other people, like you, Jason—through a set of circumstances—are left without family other than in name. Those people have to go out and create family."

As I was leaning back in contemplation of Red Stevens' powerful words, the intercom on my desk buzzed. I pressed the button and said, "Yes," and heard the always able and efficient voice of my court reporter, Scott, say, "Your Honor, we're all gathered in the conference room for lunch."

"I'm on my way," I responded, hoping that he didn't realize I had forgotten.

For many years, I had hosted a monthly luncheon for my courtroom colleagues, and the luncheon date was today. I rushed into the conference room generally reserved for judges and lawyers but also the site of my monthly luncheons. I took my seat at the head of the table beneath the portrait of my treasured late mentor and friend Judge Eldridge. For years, sitting in this spot, I had felt his presence and somehow believed it to be fitting that Judge Eldridge was a part of our monthly luncheons.

Seated to my right was Paul, my bailiff. Most people consider Paul to be a virtual giant. I have never asked the exact measurement but would guess that his height is probably closer to seven feet than it is to six feet. The fact that he is an imposing figure has helped us many times in the courtroom when we are confronted with particularly agitated or even potentially violent people. Although we all know Paul wouldn't hurt a fly, somehow his presence has kept us out of a number of uncomfortable situations.

Seated to Paul's right was my other bailiff, Jim. If Paul is imposing and intimidating, Jim is accommodating and a calming presence everywhere he goes. He seems to understand people at a deep level and be able to communicate with them. I have seen him over the years subdue many angry litigants with nothing more than a calming smile and a kind word.

Across the table from the bailiffs and seated directly to my left was my longtime court reporter, Scott. As we were preparing to eat our lunch, Scott was organizing all of his pills and various medications that he constantly took for his ongoing fight with cancer. When we all heard that Scott had been diagnosed with cancer, everyone was devastated and distraught. Everyone except for Scott, that is. He has shown a grace, a dignity, and a perseverance that has kept me in constant awe.

As we began to eat, the discussion flowed from our families to sports and even politics. We shared many common emotions and experiences as a result of being in the constant firing line together inside the courtroom. In a way that would be hard to explain, it is almost like we have been to war together. We trust each other and understand each other at a deep and significant level.

As my three colleagues were bantering back and forth in a good-natured way, I sat back—along with Judge Eldridge above me—and simply enjoyed being in their company.

As our luncheon time drew to an end and the afternoon's session in court loomed, my thoughts returned to Red Stevens and his words about the unique and wonderful nature of family. As I pushed away from the table, I realized that—right here in this special room around this special table—we had somehow formed our own family.

———

Back in the courtroom, I called the proceedings to order and directed my comments toward L. Myron Dudly and the Stevens family.

"The court does, indeed, appreciate the arguments of counsel for the Stevens family and agrees that Jason Stevens has little or no experience in what anyone would define as a traditional family."

Murmurs of excitement rocketed through that side of the courtroom as the family anticipated victory.

"On the other hand, after reviewing Red Stevens' thoughts and beliefs surrounding The Gift of Family, a wonderful, natural family experience—while priceless—is not necessary."

I glanced toward Jason and Hamilton across the aisle and ruled. "This court finds that, while unique and unconventional, Jason Stevens has demonstrated an understanding of The Gift of Family as defined by Red Stevens. He will be given the customary thirty days to demonstrate his ability to pass this gift on to other people in need of all the things family can bring."

———

During the next month, I thought about the concept of family in new ways. I was more thankful for my biological family and more aware of and grateful for my work family and the other people who make my life so special.

Jason was back on the stand, and Hamilton had directed him

to explain his actions during the last month surrounding helping others understand The Gift of Family.

Jason explained, "I thought a long time about different people I have come in contact with who need the things family can bring. The kids at the Saturday School in the park don't all have good home lives, but Tom and everyone at the Saturday School seem to be beginning to fill in that role. The single moms have been struggling for a stable family life, but the day-care co-op and the things they are doing together are really making a difference. So, I decided to focus on the seven families Alexia and I helped who had lost or were losing children.

"Since last month, we've been contacted about even more families facing that horrible situation. We organized a brief and informal support-group session so that the pain, the joy, and the lessons learned could be spread among all the hurting families.

"It went over really well, so we are going to make it a monthly event. A lot of the families who lost children a number of months ago are able to begin helping those who are just beginning to face the reality of the struggles before them. These families who are being torn apart are able to come together and begin to find a way to try and fill the tremendous void left behind in a family when a child is gone."

Hamilton had no further questions and turned it over to Mr. Dudly.

Dudly inquired, "Are any of these people related in any way?"

"No," Jason responded. "Not other than the fact that they are sharing the same pain and suffering."

"So, really," Dudly questioned, "you have possibly started a successful support group and, as worthwhile as this may be, how can you call this a family?"

Jason paused for several seconds then spoke with conviction. "My grandfather believed, and I believe, that a family is nothing more or less than people in our lives that provide the love, support, and encouragement that we all want and need from a family."

Dudly dismissed Jason and spoke directly to me before I made my ruling.

Dudly pleaded, "Your Honor, this court must rule on behalf of my clients on this point of law as it pertains to The Gift of Family outlined in Red Stevens' last will and testament. While Mr. Jason Stevens may be accomplishing some laudable work, it could not in any way be called or defined as helping people with The Gift of Family.

"These people ..." Dudly pointed toward his side of the courtroom. "... are family in every sense of the word, and they deserve to be recognized as such by having this court restore their family assets to them."

I thanked Mr. Dudly for presenting his motion, nodded in thanks to Mr. Hamilton, and spoke for the record.

"The court agrees that Jason Stevens has not been working in an area that would generally be defined as family. It does not meet the legal definition of family as well; however, it does meet Red Stevens' definition of family as he intended it for his grandson in The Gift of Family. This court rules in favor of Jason Stevens and will be recessed until 10:00 a.m. tomorrow when we consider The Gift of Laughter."

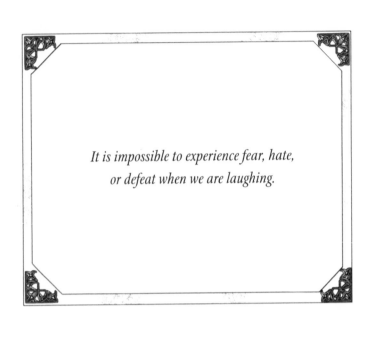

It is impossible to experience fear, hate,
or defeat when we are laughing.

NINE

THE LIFE OF LAUGHTER

After the final decision on The Gift of Family, I returned to my chambers to clean up a bit of paperwork. I was going to stay downtown at the court building and wait for my hot dinner date for the evening to arrive. Marie and I feel that our relationship has stayed as fun and exciting as it was in the beginning because we talk and go out on dates just like we did from the start.

I had almost completed the voluminous pile of paperwork the clerks had placed before me when Marie came through the mahogany door.

She smiled and said, "Your Honor, you'd better be on your best behavior this evening, because I have another offer."

I smiled and inquired, "What kind of offer are we talking about?"

"Well," she explained, "when I came into the court building, there was a new guard on duty downstairs, and he didn't know me. I told him I was here for a dinner date, and he said he would be off in forty-five minutes if I wouldn't mind waiting."

I pounded on my ridiculous judicial desk as if using my gavel and exploded in mock anger, "I'll have that man's job!"

Marie laughed raucously and said, "Your Honor, I don't think you'd make a good guard, and I don't think anyone would trust you with a loaded weapon. You'd better stick with this judge gig you've got going here."

Marie asked me how my day in court had gone, so I told her all about the Stevens' case and The Gift of Family.

Marie asked, "So what's next on that case?"

I explained that in the morning we would be looking into The Gift of Laughter that Red Stevens had outlined for Jason in his last will and testament.

Marie was curious and asked how I knew exactly what Red Stevens wanted for his grandson. I told her about the videos that Red had made to deliver the various gifts to Jason after Red's death.

Marie asked, "How does that work exactly?"

I considered for a minute, picked up the DVD marked *The Gift of Laughter*, and replied, "Well, I'll show you. Or better yet, Red Stevens will show you."

I slid the disk into the player, and Red Stevens appeared. I pressed *pause* so I could get back to my chair, and Marie could settle into one of my guest chairs.

She stared at Red Stevens on the screen and asked, "How long before his death was this video made?"

"As I understand it, it was completed just a few weeks before his passing," I responded.

Marie thought aloud, "It's really rather sad that someone has to talk to a video camera instead of their grandson when they're so near the end of life."

I considered her perspective then said, "It's sad, but I believe Red knew that this was the only way he had a chance of reaching Jason."

As silence fell over my chambers, I finally pushed *play*, and Red shared his thoughts and feelings with Jason.

"This month, you are going to learn about The Gift of Laughter. The Gift of Laughter I want you to learn about is not a comedian in a nightclub or a funny movie. It is the ability to look at yourself, your problems, and life in general and just laugh. Many people live unhappy lives because they take things too seriously. I hope you have learned in the last six months that there are things in life to be serious about and to treasure, but life without laughter is not worth living.

"This month, I want you to go out and find one example of a person who is experiencing difficulties or challenges in his or her life but who maintains the ability to laugh. If a person can laugh in the face of adversity, that individual will be happy throughout life."

Marie and I walked arm-in-arm out of the court building, through the urban park, and toward our favorite Greek restaurant. We remembered times past, both good and bad, and laughed at them all. Some of the worst times we had experienced financially, and the hardships we endured, now just seem petty and humorous. We enjoyed a wonderful dinner and listened to the life-affirming Greek music provided by a strolling violinist.

Near the end of the evening, I excused myself and went to the restroom. I returned shortly and slipped back into my place at the table. I will never in my life figure out how she did it, but when I looked across at Marie, she lowered her dessert menu and there before me sat my beloved bride wearing a giant rubber nose, a goofy fake mustache, and ridiculous comedy glasses.

She said with total dignity and solemnity, "Your Honor, may it please the court, this is your Gift of Laughter."

I heard Paul intone the always-familiar "All rise."

I made my way up the three stairs as I had done countless thousands of times. I often thought I could do this in my sleep if ever called upon to do so. I settled into my chair and pounded the gavel, calling the court to order. I realized that there needed to be a certain amount of pomp and circumstance surrounding my duties as a judge, but Marie's Gift of Laughter was still in my memory, so it was hard to take myself too seriously.

I greeted Mr. Hamilton and asked him to open the proceedings. He steered Jason through his testimony of how Red Stevens had required Jason to go out and find someone who was experiencing struggles or difficulty in their life but dealt with it through laughter. Jason explained how he had met his friend David Reese, a blind young man, who dealt with his blindness and everything else in life through his humor.

Mr. Hamilton dismissed Jason, who stepped down from the stand, then Hamilton called on David Reese to testify.

A handsome young man wearing dark glasses and using a white cane moved confidently and quickly toward the witness stand. He tapped his cane on the one step up into the witness box and then negotiated it deftly. He slid into the witness chair, and my bailiff, Jim, asked him to place his hand on the Bible. David Reese did so and swore to tell the truth, the whole truth, and nothing but the truth, then Theodore J. Hamilton approached and said, "Hello, Mr. Reese. Thank you for being here today."

David Reese smiled and said, "It's good to see you again, Mr. Hamilton. In fact, as I always say, it's good to see anybody."

Tentative laughter could be heard filtering through the courtroom.

David continued. "I don't know who designed that step up into the witness box, but I'll bet it wasn't a blind guy."

David faced directly toward Hamilton and said, "Another great tie, Mr. Hamilton. How many of those do you have?"

The laughter built and rose pleasantly in my courtroom until Dudly shouted, "Your Honor, we most vigorously object to this slapstick comedy routine that opposing counsel has obviously orchestrated."

"I didn't know we had an orchestra," David shot back. He asked, "And who is this guy? Is he with the string section?"

Dudly became indignant and announced, "Young man, I am L. Myron Dudly of Dudly, Cheetham, and Leech."

David laughed and quipped, "Wow, people like you are hard on a poor blind guy like me trying to spread a little cheer. I have to work at making people laugh at me, and it just comes naturally to you."

The laughter roared about us, and David Reese asked, "Is that your real name, or did you hire comedy writers?"

I chuckled, myself, but finally had to pound my gavel and call for order.

I addressed David Reese. "Mr. Reese, while your humor may be a breath of fresh air here in my courtroom, and even though we are exploring The Gift of Laughter, I will have to ask you to confine yourself to the questions addressed to you by counsel."

David Reese smiled innocently, shrugged his shoulders, and nodded, saying, "Good enough. Let's do this thing."

Hamilton resumed questioning. "Mr. Reese, is it true that as a result of Jason Stevens' search for The Gift of Laughter as directed by Red Stevens, he met you on a subway train?"

"Yes, sir, that is correct-a-mundo."

Dudly began to rise, and I glared at him, motioning for him to be seated.

Hamilton continued. "From that time to this, have you formed a relationship with Jason Stevens?"

David nodded and said, "Absolutely."

"What is the nature of your relationship?" Hamilton inquired.

"Well, we're friends. We get together from time to time and talk on the phone a lot. Jason met with me and some of my students at the school for the blind just recently. We know different people and move in different circles, so we kind of exchange jokes with one another. When I see something funny— no pun intended—or Jason finds something good, we share it."

"And why is humor important in your life?" Hamilton asked.

David Reese sighed deeply and was serious for the first time that day. "Sometimes laughter and my humor is all I have. Being blind can be depressing and unbelievably difficult. People don't know how to deal with you, and they're afraid of saying or doing something wrong, so they just avoid you. But laughter is the universal language. It's just like here in the courtroom today. I'm sure a lot of people were nervous and didn't know what to think when I walked up here wearing my shades and using my white cane. But a couple of jokes later, and we're all comfortable and, well, we're just friends."

Mr. Hamilton thanked David for his appearance and stated, "Your Honor, I have no further questions for this witness.

Mr. Dudly got to his feet and began. "Mr. Reese, do you have any psychological training in your background?"

David laughed and responded, "No, but I have been to a psychologist; however, I was more of the thera*pee* and not the thera*pist*."

A few chuckles could be heard from the gallery, but Dudly ignored them and continued. "Would you say Jason Stevens has helped you better understand or deal with your situation through laughter?"

David responded, "Jason is my friend, and we laugh together. We all deal with our own situations, but sometimes it's nice to have someone who cares enough to share a good laugh."

David paused and then asked, "Does anyone ever call you Dud?"

I joined in the laughter that overflowed the courtroom. Mr. Dudly was beet red and shaking. He stammered and pointed his finger at me, then Mr. Hamilton, and finally David Reese before he simply sat down. When order was restored, I inquired of Mr. Dudly if he had any further questions. He shook his head vigorously with disgust and busied himself with some paperwork in front of him.

I addressed myself to my court reporter, Scott, saying, "Let the record show that the court finds that Jason Stevens has demonstrated he understands The Gift of Laughter as set forth in the last will and testament of Howard 'Red' Stevens. Thirty days from today, we will rule upon Jason Stevens' ability to share his Gift of Laughter with others. This court stands adjourned."

———————

In the intervening month, either there were a lot more humorous episodes in my life than normal, or exploring The Gift of Laughter through Red Stevens and Jason had made me more aware of all the opportunities to enjoy laughter.

"Let the record show that today the court will be ruling on the matter pertaining to Red Stevens' last will and testament relating to Jason Stevens' ability to pass on The Gift of Laughter."

I waved toward Theodore J. Hamilton and asked, "Mr. Hamilton, can you get the ball rolling for us here this morning?"

"I would be pleased to, Your Honor."

Hamilton waved Jason toward the witness stand. Jason settled in, and Hamilton inquired, "Jason, in the last month, have you had an opportunity to pass along The Gift of Laughter that your grandfather shared with you?"

Jason nodded emphatically and began. "Yes. I thought a lot about The Gift of Laughter and who might need it the most. When I visited the senior citizens' center to see how the periodic calls from the students at the school for the blind were going, I felt I had my answer.

"The senior citizens at the center are often suffering from chronic physical pain, and many of them have lost a spouse and a great number of their lifelong friends. They don't get to see their children or grandchildren as often as they wish, so I felt they needed The Gift of Laughter."

Hamilton prompted, "So how did you facilitate this?"

Jason continued. "Well, after breakfast each day at the center, a lot of the senior citizens gather together in regular groups around the television or on the sun porch or just in the hall near one another's rooms. I went around to each of these groups and let them know that we had a new activity called the Monday Morning Circle of Laughter."

Jason paused and then explained, "These senior citizens had gotten into the habit of getting together each morning and sharing complaints, fears, or just their aches and pains; but I told them from now on, Mondays were dedicated to the Circle of Laughter.

"All of the informal groups would allow each senior citizen, in turn, to share something humorous that had happened to them recently or a funny memory they have from the past. Nothing other than humor is allowed on Mondays."

Hamilton nodded and asked, "So what have the results been from this Circle of Laughter?"

"It's really been amazing," Jason explained as he reached inside his jacket and drew out an envelope. "Here is a letter from the senior citizens' center's administrator. She explains that they are compiling data from the doctors and nurses, but the preliminary results have shown that the residents rest better, require less medication, and report an overall improved sense of well-being on Mondays than other days of the week. One of the physicians is actually planning to produce a report for a geriatric medical journal outlining the success of the Circle of

Laughter."

Hamilton thanked Jason and spoke to Mr. Dudly. "He's all yours."

Dudly nodded perfunctorily and began. "Mr. Stevens, did you actually teach these senior citizens anything about humor or laughter?"

Jason shook his head and admitted, "No, not really."

"Did you facilitate or lead the discussions in these groups?" Dudly asked.

"No, not really," Jason stated.

Dudly began to pace and shook his head as if disappointed in Jason's answer then asked, "So other than suggesting that these people get together and discuss laughter, what did you really accomplish?"

"Nothing," Jason said. "My grandfather taught me—and I realize—that humor exists in all of us. It surrounds us every day. Potential laughter is everywhere if we just find it and share it, but as my grandfather taught me through The Ultimate Gift, unless we look for and expect all of the good things and gifts of life, we will miss them. I simply helped a group of people focus on laughter instead of pain, suffering, and loneliness."

Mr. Dudly waved at Jason and mumbled, "Dismissed."

Dudly focused on me and said, "Your Honor, it is clear that Jason Stevens did not pass on or bring anyone The Gift of Laughter. These people at the center had it all along. I ask this court to rule on behalf of my clients, the rightful heirs to Red Stevens' fortune."

I nodded as Dudly returned to his seat and stated for all present to hear, "Mr. Dudly, I agree with you ..."

Excited whispers could be heard from the Stevens family.

I tapped my gavel and began again. "I agree with you in that Jason didn't bring these senior citizens anything they didn't already have, but as I have come to understand Red Stevens' intentions with respect to The Gift of Laughter, the fact that Jason allowed them to understand and express the laughter inside of them may, indeed, be the greatest gift of all."

I rapped my gavel and ruled, "This court finds in favor of Jason Stevens. We will resume tomorrow and consider The Gift of Dreams."

Dreams are the essence of all we can become.

TEN

THE LIFE OF DREAMS

The next morning found me—with cup of coffee in hand—leaning back in my comfortable leather chair and staring out the window toward the east in time for the sunrise. While I was in my usual place, the sun wasn't. Or at least I could not have sworn to it under oath in a court of law. There was a filmy layer of clouds and fog lying atop the city. The most solid and permanent structures looked temporal as viewed from the window in my chambers that morning.

Reality is not always easy to define, and everything is not as it appears. These are good things for a presiding judge to remember both personally and professionally.

I held the DVD labeled *The Gift of Dreams* in my hand as I contemplated the ironies of life and what Red Stevens might reveal about dreams. The familiar image of Howard "Red" Stevens materialized on the video screen.

"Jason, this month you're going to learn about a gift that

belongs to all great men and women—The Gift of Dreams. Dreams are the essence of life—not as it is, but as it can be. Dreams are born in the hearts and minds of very special people, but the fruit of those dreams becomes reality and can be enjoyed by the whole world.

"You may not know it, but Theodore Hamilton is known far and wide as the best lawyer in the country. I know that performing at that level was a dream of his when I met him, and he has been living that dream for over fifty years. The dream came true in his heart and mind before it came true in reality.

"I can remember wandering through the swamps of Louisiana, dreaming about becoming the greatest oil and cattle baron in Texas. That dream became such a part of me that when I achieved my goals, it was like going home to a place I had never been before.

"I have been trying to decide, as I have been formulating this Ultimate Gift for you, which of the gifts is the greatest. If I had to pick one, I think I would pick The Gift of Dreams because dreams allow us to see life as it can be—not as it is. In that way, The Gift of Dreams allows us to go out and get any other gift we want out of this life.

"One of the first truly great dreamers I ever met in my life had a passion to create places and things that would touch the imagination of people. This passion was with him all the days of his life. He had his share of setbacks and failures as well as many detractors. I never saw him or talked to him at a time when he didn't want to share his latest project with me. He was in the habit of creating huge dream boards that he would hang on the wall and draw out the plans for each of his projects on.

"I remember that when he was on his deathbed, he had arranged to tack the plans for his newest project onto the ceiling of his hospital room. That way, he could continue to look at his dream as he constructed it in his mind.

"A reporter came to visit him while he was in the hospital, and my friend was so weak he could barely talk. So he actually moved over and asked the reporter to lie on his bed with him so the two of them could look at the plans on the ceiling while my friend shared his dream.

"The reporter was so moved that a person would have that much passion while dealing with a serious illness in the hospital. The reporter concluded his interview, said good-bye to my friend, and left the hospital.

"My friend died later that day.

"Please do not miss the point. A person who can live his entire life with a burning passion for his dream to the extent that he shares it on his deathbed—that is a fortunate person. My friend had his dream with him all the days of his life. It continued to grow and expand. When he would reach one milestone of his dream, another greater and grander one would appear.

"In a real way, my friend taught a lot of people how to dream and imagine a better world. His name was Walt Disney.

"But let me warn you. Your dreams for your life must be yours. They cannot belong to someone else, and they must continue to grow and expand.

"I had another friend whose name you would not know. He said it was his dream to work hard and retire at age fifty. He did, indeed, work hard and achieve a degree of success in his business. He held on to that dream of retiring, but he had no passion beyond that.

"On his fiftieth birthday, a number of us gathered to celebrate both his birthday and his retirement. This should have been one of the happiest days of his life—if his dream had been properly aligned. Unfortunately, his entire adult life had been spent in his profession. That is where he had gained a lot of his pride and self-esteem. When he found himself as a relatively young man without his profession to guide him, he faced the uncertainty of retirement. It was something he thought he had always wanted, but he discovered quickly it created no life-sustaining passion for him.

"A month later, my second friend committed suicide.

"The difference between one dreamer who was still energized by his lifelong passion while on his deathbed and another dreamer whose goal was so ill-fitting for his personality that he committed suicide should be apparent to you.

"Jason, it is important that your dream belong to you. It is not a one-size-fits-all proposition. Your dream should be a custom-fit for your personality, one that grows and develops as you do. The only person who needs to be passionate about your dream is you."

I thought about the relationship between dreams and reality in my own life. As I was contemplating my own long-held dreams—some that had come true, others that were unrealized—the sun broke through the clouds. What had been totally obscured earlier was now revealed as the most glorious sunrise I had witnessed in many months. It had been there all along.

The tension was high in my courtroom that day as Theodore Hamilton led Jason Stevens over each of the hurdles. The stakes seemed to grow even greater in this winner-take-all race to the finish.

I reminded everyone that Jason Stevens was still under oath with respect to his testimony in this case.

Mr. Hamilton began the questioning. "Jason, when your grandfather shared The Gift of Dreams with you, what was the task he asked you to undertake as a part of the process?"

Jason collected his thoughts and began. "My grandfather asked me to think about my life, my goals, and my dreams to determine what it was I wanted to accomplish in my life."

Jason fidgeted a moment in his seat, put his hand on his forehead in concentration, and then looked above the gallery. He seemed to be focused on that time and place in the past.

"I thought about a million things I could do with my life, but when I boiled them all down, they seemed to each take the same direction."

Hamilton nodded in understanding and encouraged Jason. "Please share that direction with us this morning."

"Well, it's pretty simple in a way," Jason responded. "I want to help deprived young people. I don't simply mean young people who don't have money or who come from difficult circumstances; but I want to help those who don't understand all the things that they have in their lives. I guess, in simplest terms, I want to spend my life sharing The Ultimate Gift with everyone I can."

Hamilton smiled and said, "Thank you for sharing that, Jason. That's what your grandfather wanted for you as well."

"I object," Dudly thundered. "It is for this court to decide what Red Stevens' intentions were, not Mr. Hamilton."

Hamilton mocked Dudly with a brief bow and formally

intoned, "Very well, counselor, I shall leave this witness to you, and we will allow this court to decide."

Dudly moved toward the witness box and actually leaned over the rail toward Jason.

"Mr. Stevens, doesn't it seem a little too convenient for the dream you have for your own life to be to help other people with The Ultimate Gift? Could it be that you simply want control of several billion dollars?"

Jason smiled and said, "I have been sharing The Ultimate Gift with everyone I can since my grandfather gave it to me. I will be doing that for the rest of my life, no matter what else happens."

"I see," Dudly said with great skepticism. "Do you have any experience living life in poverty?" Dudly asked.

Jason shook his head and laughed, "No, quite the contrary, actually."

Dudly continued, "Do you have any experience in your life with any sort of disability or infirmity?"

Jason shook his head and replied, "No, I've been very fortunate to be healthy my whole life."

"Then how can you reasonably expect anyone to think you are the person to help others with their dreams? You can't even undertake your own dreams without your grandfather's money that should legally and morally be the property of my clients."

"Object," Hamilton said. "Your Honor, apparently Mr. Dudly wants to not only be the lawyer and the witness but judge, jury, and executioner as well."

I tapped my gavel. "Sustained."

"I have no further need to question this witness," Dudly remarked offhandedly as he confidently strode to the counsel table, smiled at his clients assembled in the first three rows, turned, and took his seat.

"A dream is quite different from reality," I began. "There need not be any evidence to support a dream for it to be valid. In fact, the aspect that makes dreams so remarkable is the fact that they are rarely, if ever, realistic. I find that Mr. Jason Stevens' dream is both reasonable and admirable in light of his grandfather's wishes and desires as outlined in Red Stevens' last will and testament."

A collective groan could be heard and felt from the gallery behind Dudly. Dudly sat open-mouthed, thinking that he had this one in the bag.

I continued, "Jason Stevens will be given a thirty-day period to demonstrate his ability to pass on The Gift of Dreams to others. This court stands adjourned."

Jason Stevens carried a sizable box with him to the witness stand and set it on the floor near his feet. Hamilton directed him to share his activities pertaining to The Gift of Dreams over the last month, and Jason spoke.

"I began the month thinking about young people who most need The Gift of Dreams. Then I realized I had ready access to a group of kids who come from impoverished, dysfunctional, and disadvantaged backgrounds."

Jason paused, looked down at the box at his feet, and continued, "I went to the Saturday School in the park, and I told all of the kids about The Gift of Dreams. We had several discussion groups and exercises. Finally, I asked each of them to write down the dreams that they have for their life."

Hamilton smiled expansively and said, "Very good. Would you be able to share some of their dreams with us today here in the courtroom?"

Jason nodded confidently and reached into the box. He pulled out a handful of papers and began. "Taylor is age eight. He wants to play shortstop for the New York Yankees. Nicole is nine, and she wants to be an astronaut. Marcus is also nine and wants to be an actor. David is eleven, and his dream is to be a successful businessman so he can buy his mom a house and car. Laurie is seven, and she wants to be president of the United States."

Hamilton interrupted, stating for the benefit of all present, "Thank you, Jason, I think that is more than enough to demonstrate your point in this matter. I have no further questions."

"Mr. Stevens," Dudly began, "what would you say are the odds of any one child growing up to play shortstop for the New York Yankees, becoming an astronaut, or—much less—being elected president of the United States?"

"I have no idea." Jason shrugged as he spoke.

Dudly fired back, "Well, wouldn't you say it's highly improbable?"

Jason considered and then said, "Yeah, maybe."

Dudly went for the throat, asking, "Then please tell the court what the point is of this entire exercise?"

Jason placed the paperwork respectfully back into his box, sat up straight, and spoke. "The point is not what these kids are dreaming. The point is that coming from their helpless and hopeless backgrounds that they have a dream at all. My grandfather taught me that dreams can grow and change. It's not as important what dream you have as it is that you have a dream."

Dudly rested his case, and I confidently ruled, "Jason Stevens has, to the satisfaction of this court, proven that he has the ability and desire to pass along The Gift of Dreams. Monday, we will consider The Gift of Giving."

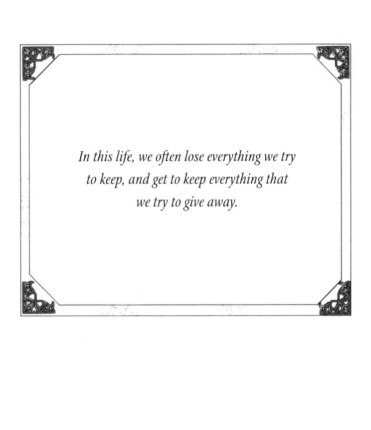

In this life, we often lose everything we try to keep, and get to keep everything that we try to give away.

ELEVEN

THE LIFE OF GIVING

The media vultures descended on the Saturday School the next morning. The obscure inner-city kids became instant celebrities across the country and around the world.

I watched an in-depth interview with nine-year-old Marcus who had a dream of being an actor. The reporters took turns shouting questions at him, flashbulbs exploded all around him, and a score of microphones were thrust in his face. Marcus was calm, cool, and collected. He handled every question as if the answer had been scripted for him, his voice never faltered, and his gaze never wavered.

At the end of his few minutes of fame, I was certain that if I were ever casting a major motion picture, Marcus would be on the top of my list.

Then Laurie appeared before the cameras. She was frail and seemed a bit bewildered. The graphic at the bottom of my TV screen reminded me that Laurie was only seven years old; but when the first question was fired at her, Laurie more than rose to the occasion.

A reporter opened with, "Laurie, what makes you want to become president?"

Laurie articulated her platform. "The street lights are out, the school needs to be painted, there are scary people on my street, and everybody is always fighting."

The reporter followed up, asking, "Well, Laurie, what are you going to do about it?"

"I'm going to change it," Laurie proclaimed in a manner that convinced me to mark my ballot for her. I wouldn't be surprised to have the opportunity to vote for Laurie in the future.

The weekend offered some needed rest, but far too soon Monday rolled around, and everyone was back in their familiar places in my courtroom.

I called for order and stated, "Today, we are going to review The Gift of Giving as it was presented to Jason Stevens by his grandfather. This court will hear evidence with respect to whether Jason Stevens has an understanding and working knowledge of his grandfather's wishes regarding The Gift of Giving. As usual, we will first hear from Mr. Hamilton, representing Jason Stevens."

Jason took his place in the witness box and, as directed by Mr. Hamilton, explained that Red Stevens had challenged him—each day of the month—to find people to give gifts to that came from Jason, himself. These could not be gifts bought by the money provided to Jason by his grandfather but instead had to be something from Jason.

Hamilton inquired, "So what did you do?"

Jason said, "Well, I found things that I could get on my own or already had that I could give away."

Hamilton nodded and said, "Can you share them with us?"

Jason pulled a folded sheet of paper from his pocket. He unfolded it and read, "On the first day, I stopped at a shopping center and found a parking space on the first row. As I was getting out of my car, I noticed an elderly couple looking for a space. I backed out and allowed them to park in my space, and I parked in the back of the lot.

"On the second day, I got caught downtown in a thunderstorm. I shared my umbrella with a young lady who didn't have one. One the third day, I went to the hospital and donated a pint of blood. On day four, I called a man in my neighborhood who had told me he needed to buy new tires. I let him know there was a really good sale going on across town. On day five, I helped an elderly woman carry her packages to her car. On day six, I agreed to watch a neighbor's children for her while she went out with some friends. On day seven, I went to the Center for the Blind and read articles to visually impaired students. On day eight, I served lunch at the soup kitchen, and on day nine I wrote a note and sent a poem to a friend.

"On day ten, I agreed to take my neighbor's kids to school. On day eleven, I helped box and move donated items for the Salvation Army. On days twelve and thirteen, I let some visiting foreign exchange students stay in my home. On day fourteen, I helped a local Scout troop with their weekly meeting. On day fifteen, I found a man with a dead battery and jump-started his car. On day sixteen, I wrote letters for several people who were in the hospital. On day seventeen, I went to the local animal shelter and walked several of their dogs in the park. On day eighteen, I gave the frequent flyer miles I had earned with an airline to a high school band planning a trip to a parade in California. Day nineteen, I worked with a local service organization and delivered meals to disabled people.

"Days twenty, twenty-one, twenty-two, and twenty-three, I took a group of inner-city kids who had never been camping and fishing on a trip with the Scout troop. I had never been camping or fishing either. On day twenty-four, I helped a local church with their rummage sale. Days twenty-five and twenty-six, I worked with a crew on a Habitat for Humanity house. Day twenty-seven, I let a local charity group use my home for a reception. Day twenty-eight, I helped one of my neighbors rake the leaves out of his yard. Day twenty-nine, believe it or not, I helped to bake cookies for the elementary school's bake sale."

Theodore J. Hamilton actually applauded as he stood in front of the witness box. He said, "Very impressive, son, but what did you do on day thirty?"

Jason chuckled and replied, "Well, Mr. Hamilton, if you'll remember I gave some of the leftover cookies I had baked for the bake sale to you and Miss Hastings."

"Yes, you did," Hamilton remarked. "And I can attest to the fact that they were quite delicious. No more questions."

Hamilton retreated to his seat as Dudly prepared to attack.

"Mr. Stevens, what would you say—in your opinion—was

the combined monetary value of all the gifts on your little list there?" Dudly pointed to Jason's paper as if it were unclean.

Jason looked bewildered, shrugged, and said, "Well, sir, I don't have any idea."

Dudly pressed. "Wouldn't you agree that most of those items had little, if any, relative worth in the real world?"

"Probably," Jason admitted.

"Then how can you hope to manage several billion dollars, based on that?" Dudly jabbed his finger toward the page in Jason's hand.

Jason pondered for several moments then said, "My grandfather told me to give away things I had gotten on my own. I didn't have any choice but to give away a part of myself." Jason paused, found his stride, and continued. "But I think it's a lot easier to manage money than it is to manage ourselves."

Dudly looked at Jason and appeared shocked. "You have got to be kidding." He looked at the ceiling and held out his hands palm upward as if he were imploring the heavens for relief from this absurdity.

I finally had to interrupt the theatrics, asking, "Mr. Dudly, do you have any other questions for this witness?"

Dudly intoned dramatically, "No, Your Honor. This matter seems more than clear."

Dudly sat down.

I nodded to Jason, thanked him for his testimony, and told him he could step down. I organized my thoughts into a ruling and spoke. "The last will and testament of Howard 'Red' Stevens called for his grandson to give away something of himself each and every day for a month. It is the finding of this court that Mr. Jason Stevens duly accomplished this task.

"During the next thirty days, he will be given the opportunity to demonstrate that he can pass along The Gift of Giving to others."

My gavel sounded with finality, and I made my way through the mahogany door into the private world of my chambers. I leaned against the monstrous desk and wondered if I could think of something of myself to give away every day for a month.

I watched Red Stevens appear on the screen before me and discuss The Gift of Giving.

"This month, I want you to learn about The Gift of Giving. This is another one of those paradoxical principles like we talked about several months ago. Conventional wisdom would say that the less you give, the more you have. The converse is true. The more you give, the more you have. Abundance creates the ability to give; giving creates more abundance. I don't mean this simply in financial terms. This principle is true in every area of your life.

"It is important to be a giver and a receiver. Jason, financially, I have given you everything that you have in this world. But, I violated the principle involved in The Gift of Giving. I gave you money and things out of a sense of obligation not a true spirit of giving. You received those things with an attitude of entitlement and privilege instead of gratitude. Our attitudes have robbed us both of the joy involved in The Gift of Giving.

"It is important when you give something to someone that it be given with the right spirit, not out of a sense of obligation. I've learned to give to people my whole life. I cannot imagine being deprived of the privilege of giving things and part of myself to other people.

"One of the key principles in giving, however, is that the gift must be yours to give—either something you earned or created or maybe, simply, part of yourself."

———

During that whole month, I looked at giving and receiving in ways I never had.

Even though I had seen it once before, the sight still amazed me. I took my seat in the courtroom, pounded my gavel, and called the court to order. I smiled at everyone assembled and said, "I want to welcome everyone to these proceedings. The law is a sacred part of our lives and culture. I'm always glad to see people participate in the process."

Once again, running from front to back on either side of my courtroom and standing shoulder to shoulder against the back wall were the single moms who had appeared in my courtroom once before during The Gift of Money hearing.

I motioned to Mr. Hamilton and Jason Stevens, and they took their places and opened the proceedings.

Hamilton inquired, "Jason, over the past month, have you had the opportunity to share The Gift of Giving as outlined by your grandfather, Howard 'Red' Stevens, with other people?"

Jason nodded and said, "Yes."

"Please fill us in on your progress," Hamilton said.

Jason gazed down the long line of single women who made an amazing silent statement just by being there, then he began. "I tried to think about The Gift of Giving and felt giving should be both creative and automatic. It needs to be something we constantly think about in new ways; but, on the other hand, it's important to develop the habit of giving regularly."

Jason looked up at me and said, "As you know, when we talked about The Gift of Money I set up a sort of financial class for all the single moms participating in the day-care co-op and support group. Those classes have continued, and we've learned that we should always do three things with every dollar we receive.

"We should first save some so that we will have money for hard and difficult times or special opportunities. Second, we should spend some to wisely and prudently take care of our immediate and future needs. And, finally, we should regularly and consistently give away a part of each dollar.

"When we discussed giving among the single moms, there was a lot of frustration, because they are on such tight budgets there was a feeling that they couldn't really accomplish anything with their individual gifts."

Jason smiled and looked around the perimeter of the room with anticipation.

Hamilton smiled as well and asked, "So what did you do, Jason?"

Jason announced, "All of the single moms in the group got together and pooled their money. Collectively, they have made a monthly pledge toward building a community center with day-care facilities at the Howard 'Red' Stevens Urban Park."

Jason reached into the inner breast pocket of his jacket and drew out an envelope. He continued, "Here is their first check written from the Single Moms Benevolence Fund and made out to the Howard 'Red' Stevens Urban Park Community Center."

A cheer rose from the single moms around the courtroom.

Old Judge Eldridge had always stressed to me the important

responsibility of keeping order in the court. Somehow I knew he was looking down on us and would approve of the fact that I let the applause run its full course.

Hamilton waved at the single moms, thanked Jason, and turned the witness over to Mr. Dudly.

Dudly asked, "Mr. Stevens, do you have an estimate of the cost of this community center with day-care facilities to be built at this so-called park?"

Jason displayed an impish grin and clarified. "Mr. Dudly, do you mean the Howard 'Red' Stevens Urban Park where we are going to build the community center with the day-care facilities?"

"Yes, whatever," Dudly responded impatiently.

Jason continued. "Yes, I have a preliminary estimate, and it will cost several hundred thousand dollars. We are factoring in some of the variables and details to get a final number."

"So how long will it take for ..." Dudly waved his hand at the ladies standing around the room and continued, "... you to pay for such a center with these monthly checks?"

"Not nearly as long as it would take without these checks," Jason stated.

Another cheer rose from the single moms. I halfheartedly tapped my gavel but wanted to applaud, myself.

Dudly tried to ignore the display dismissively and said, "No further questions."

I tried to look each of the single moms in the eye as I slowly gazed around the room.

I spoke directly to them, "Many times in this courtroom I am called upon to make a ruling because it is my sworn duty and my legal obligation. While this ruling is, indeed, my duty and obligation, it is also my distinct pleasure to acknowledge the contribution made by each of you ..." I looked at the single moms, smiled, and continued, "... in this matter and to rule on behalf of Jason Stevens in the portion of this case relating to The Gift of Giving."

As I dismissed the court, a third and more rousing cheer erupted.

It had been a good day.

Gratitude provides a balance between the things we have and those we want.

TWELVE

THE LIFE OF GRATITUDE

One of the cable news channels carried a live remote broadcast of the groundbreaking ceremonies for the community center and day-care complex in the Howard "Red" Stevens Urban Park. Jason spoke briefly but allowed the spotlight to shine on the group of single moms who had committed funds and the residents of the community who had built the park.

I will never forget a statement made by one of the single moms. She timidly approached the lectern, stared into the blinding TV lights, and said, "In a lot of ways, life has not been kind to me. I have three children, aged two, five, and seven, and I work two jobs just to make ends meet. This park has become a safe haven where my kids and I can come to play and just spend time together. The community center with day-care facilities will mean my family—and others to come—will have opportunities that have just not been around for us.

"But more important than the change in the neighborhood is the change that has taken place inside of me. I have spent many bitter years waiting for someone else to do something for me. Now I get up every day and think about what I can do for myself and what I can do for others around me."

From my chamber window, I could view the park in the distance with the crowd surrounding the temporary platform and a number of satellite trucks ringing the perimeter. It made me think about the possibilities for my own life. It would be hard to calculate the difference we can make in the world if we simply select a goal, make a beginning, and keep on going.

In preparation for my day in court, I located the DVD marked *The Gift of Gratitude*. I slid it into the player as I anticipated Red Stevens' message for his grandson.

"When you prepare your will and a video like this, you automatically have to think about your entire life. I have been so many places and experienced so many things, it is hard to remember that I have only lived one lifetime.

"I remember, as a young man, being so poor that I had to do day labor for food to eat and had to sleep along the side of the road. I also remember being in the company of kings and presidents and knowing all of the material things this life has to offer. As I look back, I am thankful for it all.

"During what, at the time, I considered to be some of my worst experiences, I gained my fondest memories.

"Jason, this month, you are going to learn a lesson that encompasses something that has been totally lacking in your life. That is gratitude.

"I have always found it ironic that the people in this world who have the most to be thankful for are often the least thankful, and somehow the people who have virtually nothing, many times live lives full of gratitude.

"While still in my youth, shortly after going out on my own to conquer the world, I met an elderly gentleman who today would be described as homeless. Back then, there were a lot of people who rode the rails, traveling throughout the country doing just a little bit of work here and there in order to get by. It was during the Depression, and some of these so-called hobos or tramps were well educated and had lives full of rich experiences.

"Josh and I traveled together for almost a year. He seemed very old at that time, but since I was still in my teens, I may have had a faulty perspective. He is one of the only people I ever met of whom I could honestly say, 'He never had a bad day.' Or if he did, there was certainly no outward sign of it. Traveling about as we did, we often found ourselves wet, cold, and hungry. But Josh never had anything but the best to say to everyone we met.

"Finally, when I decided to settle down in Texas and seek my fortune there, Josh and I parted company. Settling down was simply not a priority in his life. When we parted, I asked him why he was always in such good spirits. He told me that one of the great lessons his mother had left him was the legacy of The Golden List.

"He explained to me that every morning before he got up, he would lie in bed—or wherever he had been sleeping—and visualize a golden tablet on which was written ten things in his life he was especially thankful for. He told me that his mother had done that all the days of her life and that he had never missed a day since she shared about The Golden List with him.

"Well, as I stand here today, I am proud to say I haven't missed a day since Josh shared the process with me almost sixty years ago. Some days I am thankful for the most trivial things, and other days I feel a deep sense of gratitude for my life and everything surrounding me.

"Jason, today, I am passing the legacy of The Golden List on to you. I know that it has survived well over one hundred years simply being passed from Josh's mother through Josh to me, and now to you. I don't know how Josh's mother discovered the process, so its origins may go back much further than I know.

"In any event, I am passing it on to you, and if you will be diligent in the beginning, before long it will simply become a natural part of your life, like breathing."

Once again, I called the court to order in the matter of the last will and testament of Howard "Red" Stevens. After the formalities were out of the way and Jason Stevens had taken the stand, the legendary Theodore J. Hamilton went to work.

"Jason, isn't it true that—as a part of your grandfather's bequest of The Ultimate Gift to you—he taught you about The Gift of Gratitude?"

Jason nodded and replied, "Yes, sir."

Hamilton continued. "Isn't it also true that Red Stevens shared with you a process called The Golden List?"

Once again, Jason nodded in agreement and said, "Yes, sir."

Hamilton smiled as if understanding and asked, "Could you please share with this court about the process of The Golden List."

Jason nodded, cleared his throat, and began. "My grandfather told me about a process he had learned many years before that had made his life better. Each day, you simply think of ten things that you are thankful for."

Hamilton inquired, "Did you perform this task within the thirty days allotted to you for The Gift of Gratitude?"

"Yes, sir," Jason confirmed.

Hamilton retrieved a page from his counsel table and returned to Jason, asking, "I have here a copy of the list you made of the things you were thankful for during your Gift of Gratitude month."

Hamilton held the list out in front of Jason and said, "Can you please confirm for the court that this is a copy of the list you made in your own handwriting?"

Jason looked over the list carefully, glanced up at me, and stated, "That's my list."

Dudly interrupted, "I'll take a look at that, if you don't mind."

"Be my guest," Hamilton said with mock cordiality.

L. Myron Dudly glared at the page in contempt, retorted, "Whatever," and stomped back to his seat.

Hamilton slipped his out-of-date reading glasses onto his nose and held the page at arm's length. "I see here on that day you were thankful for your friends, your family, and The Ultimate Gift, among other things."

Hamilton looked up at Jason over the reading glasses and asked, "Does that seem right to you?"

"Yes, sir," Jason confirmed.

Hamilton folded his glasses and put them into their ancient leather case. He glanced up at me and said, "That will be all, Your Honor."

I waved at Dudly.

L. Myron Dudly approached the witness box as if he were a homerun hitter who needed several runs in the late innings.

"Mr. Stevens, would it be true that for the majority of your life you took your wealth, position, prestige, and opportunities provided by your grandfather totally for granted?"

"That's true," Jason admitted.

"Furthermore," Dudly pressed, "isn't it true that during his life you never once thanked your grandfather and actually were ashamed of him to an extent that you wouldn't even claim him as your grandfather but wanted to palm him off as some kind of distant great uncle or something?"

Jason sighed and slowly nodded his head, stating, "Yes, that's right."

Dudly shook his head as if disappointed in an unruly child and inquired, "Then how can you expect this court to believe you understand gratitude because you made up one little list of things anyone should be grateful for on one particular day?"

"It wasn't one day," Jason replied defiantly. "I have a Golden List for every day."

Dudly exhibited false shock, saying in a ridiculous falsetto voice, "Well, excuse me. I guess you feel qualified to manage several billion dollars because you wrote down a list every day that month."

Jason shook his head and reported, "No, I have made a Golden List every day since my grandfather shared the idea with me."

Dudly laughed mockingly and asked incredulously, "You want to sit there and have us believe that every day since your grandfather's death, well over a year ago, you have taken the time to mentally formulate a list of ten things for which you are grateful?"

Jason reached inside his jacket as he spoke. "I not only

thought about what I was grateful for, but I wrote it down."

A worn leather diary could be seen in Jason's hand. He held it lovingly.

Dudly quickly masked the shock he felt and said, "Let me see that book."

Jason held it out toward him. Dudly flipped through a few pages and sighed as if feeling great impatience and frustration.

"Mr. Stevens, you want to tell this court, under oath, with penalty of perjury, that you have written in that book ten things you're thankful for every day since the time your grandfather presented you with the idea of The Gift of Gratitude?"

Jason shook his head and said, "No, sir."

Dudly slapped his hands together and exclaimed, "I thought so."

But before Dudly could continue, Jason said, "This is actually my third book. The first two got filled up."

Dudly shook his head in disbelief. He said haughtily, "Well, why don't you just read us your supposed entry for today?"

Jason reverently turned the pages and began to read. "Today, I am grateful for the groundbreaking for the community center in the park. I am grateful for the single moms who made it possible. I am grateful for the people of the community who built the park. I am grateful for Jeffrey Watkins who was willing to take my case when no one else would. I am grateful for my friend David Reese who helps me keep laughing through this difficult court case.

"I am grateful for Miss Hastings for always being there for me. I am grateful for the class at the school for the blind and the people at the senior citizens' center for teaching me a lot. I am grateful for Mr. Hamilton for being my lawyer and my friend. I am grateful to Alexia for loving me when I'm not always lovable." Jason closed the book, putting it back into his pocket, concluding, "And I'm grateful to Emily for teaching me, through her dying, how I should be living."

Dudly shuffled toward his chair, mumbling, "That's all."

The silence stretched out across my courtroom. Finally, I broke it, ruling, "It is the finding of this court that Jason Stevens has adequately demonstrated The Gift of Gratitude in his life as defined by Red Stevens. We will reconvene this hearing in a month to judge his ability to pass on his Gift of Gratitude."

Before I did anything else that day, I sat at my ridiculous behemoth of a desk in my chambers and jotted down my Golden List. I called Marie to tell her that I loved her and let her know that she was number one on my list. I knew this would be a habit that would stay with me all the days of my life.

Another month had flown by. Back in my courtroom, Jason was on the stand being questioned by Mr. Hamilton.

"Jason, how did you pass along The Gift of Gratitude this month?"

Jason recounted the story. "This month was homecoming at my Ivy League university. I never exactly graduated with any particular class, so from time to time I just show up at homecoming to see a few friends I met during my time there.

"They have a banquet each year after the football game for the alumni who are back on campus. Since this court case has gotten so much media attention, the dean of the university asked me if I would like to say a few words of greeting to everyone after the meal. I got up onstage and told them all about The Gift of Gratitude and The Golden List.

"A lot of these people are like I was. They've been given everything they ever thought they wanted so they haven't gotten a lot of what they really needed. I told them that the next step toward moving into their future and getting what they want is to reach into their past and express gratitude for what they have.

"I showed them my diary." Jason patted his pocket where the diary was kept and continued. "Many of them started jotting down lists on napkins or the backs of programs. The Gift of Gratitude I presented received a standing ovation."

Hamilton smiled and nodded confidently and then inquired, "And then what happened, Jason?"

"Well, it was a few days later that I got a call from the president of the Alumni Association. Every year, they raise money for scholarships. This year, they have endowed the Red Stevens Memorial Scholarship—which will be awarded each year—to a deserving student from the inner-city park Saturday School."

"Thank you for everything, Jason," Hamilton said warmly.

I looked toward L. Myron Dudly and the assembled legal team from Dudly, Cheetham, and Leech. Arrayed behind them were the various assorted members of the Stevens clan. There seemed to be a lot of anxiety among the entire group. It was as if they realized that the time on the ticking clock of their case, representing billions of dollars, was rapidly running out.

Dudly shakily stood and croaked, "No questions."

I stated for the record, "Hearing no opposition, this court accepts Jason Stevens' presentation of The Gift of Gratitude as presented. This court stands adjourned until 10:00 a.m. tomorrow."

The ultimate life is nothing more than a series of ultimate days. Today's the day!

THIRTEEN

THE LIFE OF A DAY

I could feel the marathon known as The Red Stevens Last Will and Testament Case approaching the finish line; but as any great marathoner will tell you, just before the final phase of the twenty-six-mile ordeal, you hit an invisible but very real obstacle known as *the wall*. *The wall* has stolen the hopes and dreams of many a competitor.

Rex the Wonder Dog and I were taking a vigorous walk around the Howard "Red" Stevens Urban Park. Rex was expertly leading me by his leash. Since he could feel me trying to restrain him with the leash, he felt confident enough to explore any direction or change course at any time.

In life, and most certainly in walking Rex the Wonder Dog, control is an illusion. Rex and I have spent many such hours with him leading the way and me contentedly following behind. He is not nearly as young nor as fast as he used to be, but then neither am I. A veritable match made in heaven between pet and master. Rex and I just aren't sure who fills which role in that relationship.

The seasons of my life have been punctuated by first owning and then growing to love a series of loyal dogs. I have kept an informal list of things that I absurdly think I would do differently if I were King of the World. I realize that the odds of this happening are not great.

Among the many things on my list are: If I were king, we would enjoy the energy of youth when we had the wisdom of age to temper it. If I were king, winter would be shortened to a period just long enough so that we would fully appreciate spring, summer, and fall. And not the least of these, if I were king, a beloved dog would live long enough to be with you all the days of your life.

I shared with Rex my concerns and inadequate feelings surrounding the Red Stevens case. Rex listened attentively, as he always does, and looked at me with those big brown eyes that communicate, "I may not understand what you're talking about, but I know that you are more than capable of doing whatever needs to be done."

It's wonderful to have someone who always believes in you. Between Marie and Rex the Wonder Dog, I am doubly blessed.

The time finally came for me to get back to the court building and for Rex to get home and perform his unknown, but no doubt vital, tasks for the day.

———————

I had thought the courtroom had been filled to capacity during the ten months of this case, but as we entered the eleventh and next-to-last month, Jim and Paul had to set up additional folding chairs, covering every square inch of the available space.

"Good morning," I said to everyone. "Today, we are here to consider The Gift of a Day as outlined in The Ultimate Gift left as a bequest from Red Stevens to his grandson, Jason. It's all yours, Mr. Hamilton."

Theodore J. Hamilton called Jason Stevens to the stand, and I reminded Jason and everyone that his testimony was still under oath.

Hamilton began. "Mr. Stevens, were you given a lesson and an opportunity to perform tasks by your grandfather regarding The Gift of a Day?"

Jason nodded and confirmed, "Yes, I was."

"Share that experience with us," Hamilton prompted.

"My grandfather told me to think about how I would spend the last day of my life."

Hamilton smiled, encouraging Jason as he continued. "Well, I decided I wanted to get up early in the morning and think about my Golden List of things I was thankful for, but on my last day, it would be a lot longer than ten things. I would want to have a really nice breakfast with a group of friends outside on a patio. I hope we would talk about how all of us could get the most out of our day and our lives. Then I decided I would call a lot of people who have meant a great deal to me in my life and thank them—like Gus Caldwell, the people at the library in South America, and the kids at the Red Stevens Boys Home."

Jason paused, took a deep breath, and sighed heavily. He looked at his extended family members across the courtroom and said, "I decided I would like to call all of my family members, thanking them for the good times and apologizing for the bad ones. Next, I decided I would take a friend to lunch and talk about the dreams he has for his life.

"That night, I decided it would be good to have a special banquet for all my friends. I would tell them how much they meant to me and share with them all the gifts in The Ultimate Life. We would videotape the banquet so that we could share that time and message with other people as they consider their lives."

Hamilton paused and then said, "Jason, I want to thank you for sharing that."

Hamilton returned to his seat at the counsel table, and I offered Mr. Dudly an opportunity to question Jason.

"So, Mr. Stevens, let me get this straight. To prove that you understood The Gift of a Day, you made up a group of activities that you thought were important to do on your last day."

Jason nodded and confirmed, "Yes, sir."

Dudly continued. "If these items are so important that you would want to be sure you did them on your last day, how many of them have you done to date?"

Jason fidgeted for a few moments, cleared his throat nervously, and said, "Well, I haven't done them all. It's not easy to master The Gift of a Day, but I have done a lot of them. I've called and written friends I wouldn't have contacted without learning The Gift of a Day. I am more conscious about thanking everybody for what they have done for me in my life, and I have dedicated myself to passing on my grandfather's Ultimate Gift."

Dudly, sensing weakness, circled for the kill. "So, Mr. Stevens, if it is so important to pack as many things as possible into each day of our lives—and certainly the last day of our lives—can you tell us why, after your grandfather's lesson and after having a whole month to think about it, you didn't plan anything for the entire afternoon of your mythical last day of life?"

Dudly beamed triumphant, and Jason looked down at his feet and mumbled, "I did have plans for the afternoon."

"Oh, you did, did you?" Dudly stated confrontationally. "Well, if it's so important, why don't you share those plans with us now and tell us why you didn't present them when you were asked to as a part of your sworn testimony."

Jason glanced uneasily toward the counsel table, let out a long breath, and said, "More than a year ago when, through a video, my grandfather taught me about The Gift of a Day, I prioritized every minute of what I would have planned then for the last day of my life. I had intended to include plans of spending the afternoon in the park, at a museum, and out on a sailboat in the harbor."

Dudly rubbed his hands together in glee and asked, "Well, Mr. Stevens, if all that's so important, why did you fail to even mention it in your sworn statement earlier?"

"I had planned to do all those things with Emily," Jason said as a tear rolled down his cheek.

The sounds of several people softly crying could be heard as Jason continued. "But I guess what I really learned from planning my last day is the fact that everything's important because for some of us, like Emily, it really is our last day."

Dudly looked like a giant balloon that had just lost all of its air. He shook his head and plopped into his chair.

I tapped my gavel and spoke. "This court finds in favor of

Jason Stevens. We will reconvene in thirty days to conclude the matter relating to The Gift of a Day."

———————

I watched Red Stevens teaching his grandson on the screen before me.

"Jason, I want you to know that as I was contemplating the ultimate gift I wanted to present you through my will, I spent a lot of time thinking about you. I think you gained a permanent place in my Golden List each morning. I am thankful that you and I share a family heritage, and I sense a spark in you that I have always felt in myself. We are somehow kindred spirits beyond just our family ties.

"As I have been going through the process of creating my will and thinking about my life and my death, I have considered all of the elements in my life that have made it special. I have reviewed many memories, and I carry them with me like a treasure.

"When you face your own mortality, you contemplate how much of life you have lived versus how much you have left. It is like the sand slipping through an hourglass. I know that at some point I will live the last day of my life. I have been thinking about how I would want to live that day or what I would do if I had just one day left to live. I have come to realize that if I can get that picture in my mind of maximizing one day, I will have mastered the essence of living, because life is nothing more than a series of days. If we can learn how to live one day to its fullest, our lives will be rich and meaningful."

I thought about The Gift of a Day and what I would do with my last day on earth. I told the court clerk to reschedule any hearings I had the next day, and then I called Marie and told her that tomorrow was reserved for The Gift of a Day.

———— • ————

During dinner that night, we talked about all the special things we wanted to do the following day.

We were up early in the morning. We had a special breakfast and walked, talked, and enjoyed a show in the company of some special friends. That night, we watched the sunset together, as it is Marie's favorite time of the day.

As the special day drew to a close, we were both struck by the fact that—although the day had, indeed, been a gift—all of the things we did could have been done on most any other day. I knew the rest of our lives would be different because the rest of our days would be different.

———— • ————

Thirty days came and went, and Jason Stevens was back in my courtroom in the witness box. Hamilton asked him to explain how he had passed on The Gift of a Day.

Jason said, "I thought about the people that might benefit most from The Gift of a Day, and I realized it would be people who didn't have many days left.

"There is a place called The Crossroads Center run by a wonderful family. They help hospice patients experience one special day. I decided to help them with their work so more people could experience The Gift of a Day."

Jason organized his thoughts and went on. "There was a one-hundred-year-old man who wanted to ride a motorcycle. We got him in a sidecar with a helmet and goggles and toured him around the countryside. He had an amazing experience, and his picture riding in the sidecar made it into the newspapers. I think a lot of other people will begin thinking about each day as a gift.

"Then there was a terminal cancer patient who had never seen the ocean. I helped make arrangements for her to travel to the shore. She strolled up and down the beach and just looked out at the vast ocean.

"There was a person with just a few days left to live who wanted to meet a well-known singer and entertainer. I got in contact with the record company, and they made arrangements for the patient to sit on the front row at a concert and go back stage afterward to have dinner with the star.

"And, finally, I asked the Crossroads people to work with me on teaching The Gift of a Day to people who have not been diagnosed with a terminal condition. Once a week, they do a seminar on The Gift of a Day. They will be teaching it next week at the Saturday School. I think this is important for everyone."

"I do, too," Hamilton agreed and passed it on to me to tell Dudly to ask his questions.

"Mr. Stevens, if I understand your story, you didn't really help these people directly. You worked with an existing organization."

"Yes, sir," Jason stated.

"So what did you do on your own to help other people understand The Gift of a Day that your grandfather gave you?"

Jason was flustered. "I didn't do anything on my own. Just like I didn't build the park on my own. I believe my grandfather would say that The Gift of a Day is too big to pass along all by yourself, so I got some help."

Dudly asked doubtfully, "So, do you believe you have passed on The Gift of a Day, and are you convinced you have an understanding of it yourself?"

Jason chuckled and said, "About all I can say is I understand enough for today, but I'm still learning because, if I'm lucky, tomorrow will be another day."

Dudly knew he was beaten on this hurdle, and he retreated—hoping for better results later.

"Let the record show that Jason Stevens is deemed to understand and to have passed on The Gift of a Day. This court stands adjourned until 10:00 a.m. tomorrow when we will conduct a hearing on the final element—The Gift of Love."

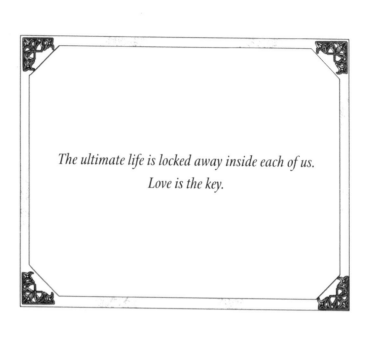

The ultimate life is locked away inside each of us.
Love is the key.

FOURTEEN

THE LIFE OF LOVE

The TV networks were carrying around-the-clock coverage of the final stages of the Red Stevens case. As I was flipping through the channels, I noticed a panel of law school professors debating the issues. It got very heated, and the only thing all of the legal scholars agreed upon was the fact that this case was like a twelve-round heavyweight championship fight. You could lose eleven rounds in a row and score a knockout punch in the twelfth and walk away with the prize.

I couldn't help but feel the gravity of what hung in the balance, dependent upon my decision. Either the entire Stevens family would lose the millions of their inheritance, or Jason would lose the control of billions that Red Stevens had set aside in trust to do good work. There just didn't seem to be any middle ground.

I spent a lot of time seeking the wisdom to find some sort of compromise, but when it was all boiled down, it seemed there was no way out other than the fact that there would be a winner and a loser. I couldn't believe that this was what Red Stevens would have wanted.

I stared at the clock in my chambers. Time seemed to stand still; but, finally, it was 10:00. I slipped on my judicial robes, paused for a brief moment of silence and reflection, and then went through the mahogany door.

As I climbed up to the bench, I could feel the tension in the room. I had never been in a situation where, financially, there was this much at stake. I wasn't sure if any other judge had either.

I settled into my chair and wondered what the results would be when I once again stood up from my seat. I pounded my gavel and declared, "Ladies and gentlemen, this court is now in session. It has been a long road for all of us to get to this final matter in the Red Stevens' Last Will and Testament Case.

"I want to thank the attorneys involved for working professionally and tenaciously to represent their various clients. I, also, want to thank my courtroom family, Jim and Paul, who ably serve this court as bailiffs, and Scott, who I believe to be the best court reporter in the business. Finally, I want to thank my mentor and friend Judge Eldridge who presided over this courtroom for many years. He gave me a priceless example and some enormous shoes to fill. I do my best each day, as I will today, to live up to the standard he set.

"All of us here today know what is at stake. Indeed, thanks to our media friends both here in the courtroom and elsewhere, everyone around the world knows what is at stake. I would still caution everyone that this is an official and legal court proceeding. I will hold each person involved to the standard of respect and order this matter deserves.

"First I will call on Mr. Theodore J. Hamilton of Hamilton, Hamilton, and Hamilton to make his case."

I locked eyes with Hamilton and said, "Sir, it is, indeed, a privilege to have you in our courtroom and in our profession."

Hamilton nodded and said in acknowledgment, "Your Honor, I want to thank you and everyone involved in this case for giving my client nothing more or less than an opportunity to plead his case and have it judged fairly."

Hamilton paused, shuffled a few papers arrayed on the table before him, and intoned, "Your Honor, once again we call Jason Stevens to the stand to give testimony in this matter."

Hamilton strode toward Jason seated in the witness box and asked, "Mr. Stevens, in the final month of the yearlong quest that your grandfather bequeathed to you in his will, did you have occasion to learn about The Gift of Love?"

Jason nodded solemnly, replying, "Yes, sir, I did."

"And did you then have the opportunity to undertake a task that would help you experience The Gift of Love for yourself?"

Once again, Jason acknowledged, "Yes, sir."

Hamilton walked back to the counsel table and stood next to his chair. He said, "Jason, can you share that experience with this court today?"

Hamilton sat down as Jason began.

"My grandfather taught me that you can't have love in one area of your life without having love in all areas of your life. So, for The Gift of Love, I was asked to consider for the month each of the gifts I had been given and how love played an integral part in each of them."

Hamilton inquired, "And Jason, were you able to complete that task successfully?"

"Yes, sir, I was," Jason responded.

Hamilton prompted, "Jason, would you share briefly how The Gift of Love played out in each gift you received from your grandfather?"

Jason thought for a minute and said, "Well, in The Gift of Work, I learned that Gus Caldwell and my grandfather had a true respect and love for one another, and I learned how important it is to love your work. In The Gift of Money, I learned that to love money is a dead-end path; but if you love people and use money, you can truly make a difference. In The Gift of Friends, I learned that in order to have a friend you've got to be a friend. You must be willing to give love before you demand to receive it. In The Gift of Learning, I found out that the love of learning is a lifelong pursuit. It simply never ends. In The Gift of Problems, I learned that—while the circumstance may be difficult or even seem impossible—when you love yourself and those around you and focus on the things you have been given, a problem viewed through love is an opportunity. In The Gift of Family, I discovered the difference between what we like and what we love. We don't always like our family, but we can always love them through every problem and circumstance.

"In The Gift of Laughter, I learned that hatred disappears when you laugh, and then love can find its way into every situation. In The Gift of Dreams, I discovered that we each have passions and destinies inside of us. Love can unlock the potential that we have on the inside. In The Gift of Giving, I found out that we should always love everyone enough to be a giver, and love is the one thing that the more you give, the more you have. It is an inexhaustible fountain. In The Gift of Gratitude, I learned that we have received many blessings in our lives, and the only way we can show true love is to be grateful for what we've been given. In The Gift of a Day, I learned that it is impossible to love life unless you love today. If we fill each day with love, we will always have enough of everything."

I couldn't believe that, with so many people in my courtroom, there was a total prolonged, absolute silence.

Eventually, Theodore J. Hamilton rose and declared, "Your Honor, I shall not diminish the power of what we have heard by going on any farther. We rest our case with respect to this matter."

I nodded to Mr. Hamilton then swung my gaze to L. Myron Dudly. I stated, "Sir, you now have the floor in this proceeding."

Dudly sat motionless for an uncomfortable length of time. I wondered if he had heard me call on him, but eventually he stood and inevitably made his way toward the witness box like a man walking his last mile. As I look back on it, I will have to admit that Dudly actually did an admirable job against formidable odds.

He cleared his throat, nodded to me, and leapt in. "Mr. Stevens, as this is your grandfather's last will and testament that is being argued and contested before this court, let's examine your relationship with him as it relates to The Gift of Love."

Dudly paced back and forth gaining confidence and momentum. "Mr. Stevens, would you say before this court that you loved your grandfather for the years of your life that he was with you?"

Jason sighed deeply, leaned forward in his chair, and explained, "I didn't know how to love anybody, including myself, until I got The Gift of Love from my grandfather, so I would have to say honestly I did not love my grandfather while he was alive."

Dudly sensed a glimmer of hope. It seemed to be somehow communicated to the Stevens family as they appeared immediately hopeful.

Mr. Dudly pounded the rail in front of Jason and thundered, "Young man, if that be the case as you have testified under oath, how in the name of all we hold to be legal, fair, and just can you say that you loved your grandfather as outlined in his Gift of Love and that you are entitled to this inheritance?"

Dudly glared at Jason, anticipating victory.

Eventually, Jason spoke. "Mr. Dudly, I will admit I did not love my grandfather when he was alive, nor did I in any way deserve the love he had for me; but somehow through his death and The Ultimate Gift he left to me, I learned to love him and everyone around me. None of us can ever deserve love. We can just treasure it and give it away."

Dudly was shaken but was still hoping for a long shot. He addressed me.

"Your Honor, we have no further questions for this individual. As he has already admitted in his sworn testimony that he never loved his grandfather during all the years of his grandfather's life, we can do nothing other than ask this court to make a swift and certain ruling on behalf of my clients and restore to them their rightful inheritance."

Dudly slid into his seat behind the counsel table. Several of his Dudly, Cheetham, and Leech colleagues patted him on the back and flashed him the victory sign. The Stevens clan collectively leaned forward in their seats with anticipation.

I was torn as I weighed the issues before me. Love is impossible to define, so it defies judgment.

I pounded my gavel and stated, "This court will take our noon recess and reconvene at 2:00 p.m."

I fled through the mahogany door into my chambers. I spoke aloud to the DVD marked *The Gift of Love* I held in my hand, saying, "Red, if you ever had anything profound to say on the subject, there's an old judge here that would really appreciate it."

I slid the final DVD into the player and welcomed Red Stevens to my chambers for the final time.

"Jason, in this last month, I'm going to introduce you to the one part of my Ultimate Gift that encompasses all of the other gifts as well as everything good you will ever do, have, or know in your life. That is The Gift of Love.

"Anything good, honorable, and desirable in life is based on love. Anything bad or evil is simply life without the love involved. Love is a misused and overused term in our society. It is applied to any number of frivolous things and pursuits; but the love I am talking about in The Gift of Love is the goodness that comes only from God. Not everyone believes or acknowledges that. And that's okay. I still know that real love comes from him—whether or not we know it.

"Jason, we've come a long way in this Ultimate Gift. I want you to know, above all, that in spite of all the mistakes I made and the many times I failed you, Jason Stevens, that your grandfather loved you."

I spoke aloud to Red Stevens on the screen. "Thank you for your help."

I hoped that somehow he knew that I would do the very best I could for his whole family.

At 2:00 sharp, I heard a brief rap on my mahogany door. It opened enough for Scott, my court reporter, to stick his head in and say, "Your Honor, they've all been sitting and waiting for almost a half hour. I've never seen anything like it."

Back in the courtroom, I prepared to deliver—if not the most important—what I knew would become the most famous judgment of my life. I tapped my gavel, but it was wholly unnecessary as the court was in order, and every eye was focused on me.

"It is the considered decision of this court that Jason Stevens did not love his grandfather at any point during Red Stevens' life. Only after his death was Red Stevens able to teach The Gift of Love to Jason, therefore making it possible for Jason Stevens to love his grandfather. Although this arrangement is highly unconventional and completely undesirable, it does meet both the letter and the intent of the last will and testament of Howard 'Red' Stevens."

It was at that point I did have to pound my gavel repeatedly for order. Shouts of protest and anger could be heard from the Stevens family. My bailiffs, Jim and Paul, materialized at the front of the courtroom, and I felt glad for their presence.

I produced an ominous stare that I leveled at those assembled in my courtroom and spoke.

"Let me be absolutely clear that we will have order in this court, or these gentlemen before you will clear this courtroom, and a few of you may have the opportunity to experience the hospitality of our official house of detention next door."

I let my words settle over everyone and concluded, "This court will stand adjourned for thirty days, during which time Jason Stevens will be given an opportunity to demonstrate that he has the ability and aptitude to pass along The Gift of Love he received from Howard 'Red' Stevens through The Ultimate Gift."

Although we had finished for that day in the courtroom, the matter was far from settled.

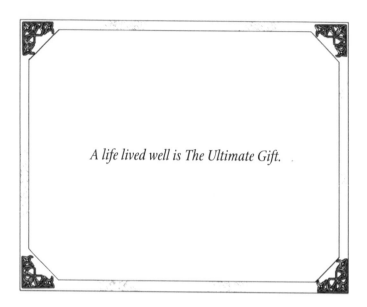

A life lived well is The Ultimate Gift.

FIFTEEN

THE ULTIMATE LIFE

I would not have believed it possible, but the media intensity increased, the tension and anxiety built, and it was hard for me or anyone else in the court building to get anything done that whole month.

Finally, it was the last day. For better or worse, it would all be finished this day. I was still searching my heart, my mind, and my soul for that elusive middle ground or some way to pull off one of Judge Eldridge's famous win/win decisions.

I pounded my gavel and called the court to order, and then it happened. The legend himself, Theodore J. Hamilton, rose and beckoned, "Your Honor, may it please the court, I have a written motion to present that has direct bearing on these proceedings."

Mr. Hamilton walked toward me holding out one single sheet of paper. L. Myron Dudly jumped to his feet and cried, "Your Honor, we object to any motions being made or heard by the court without said motion being reviewed by counsel for my clients."

Hamilton paused in mid-stride, lowered the single sheet he held in his hand, and said, "Your Honor, I beg the court's indulgence in this matter, but I will stake my entire reputation as a jurist and practitioner of the law. If Your Honor will merely review this brief document, I believe it will all become clear."

Dudly repeated, "I object."

As Hamilton began to speak, I raised my hand to both of them for silence.

"Mr. Dudly, I am going to allow this motion to be presented in this fashion, giving Mr. Hamilton the widest possible latitude based on his experience and reputation before this court."

Dudly slammed his open hand on the counsel table in frustration and dropped into his chair in resignation.

I then pointed the business end of my gavel at the one and only Theodore J. Hamilton and continued, "But, Counselor, let me warn you, if you are leading this court down an inappropriate path, I will react with every measure and course open to me to the full extent of the law."

Hamilton nodded, agreeing to the conditions, stepped forward, and handed the single sheet to me. I scanned it once then read it again and, finally, reviewed it a third time to be sure my eyes were not deceiving me.

I nodded to Mr. Hamilton and said, "This motion is accepted as presented. You may call Mr. Stevens to the stand."

Dudly sprang from his chair, knocking over a pitcher of water, and nearly upending the counsel table. He spread his arms wide, pleading, "Your Honor, there has been a motion before this court, both presented and accepted, without my clients having their right to due process in the matter."

I nodded in understanding and remarked, "Mr. Dudly, I do acknowledge your position and ask you and your clients to indulge the court for a few moments."

Jason Stevens had taken the stand, and Hamilton approached, asking, "Jason, would you please share with the court your expression of The Gift of Love as presented to you by your grandfather, Red Stevens."

Jason said, "I did not learn how to love my grandfather or anyone else in my family until, through The Ultimate Gift, I received The Gift of Love. Love both gives and receives forgiveness, so at this time, I would like to ask each member of my family to forgive me for many years of not showing them respect, much less love."

Dudly thundered, "Your Honor, that's all well and good, but ..."

I pounded my gavel and held up my other hand for Dudly to be silent.

"Your objection is overruled, counselor," I stated. I looked back down at Jason, and he continued.

"In addition to asking for forgiveness, I also wanted to ask the judge if I could try to, in some small way, express my Gift of Love to my family."

Jason looked up at me and asked, "Can I tell them?"

I nodded yes, and Jason Stevens testified.

"I asked Mr. Hamilton to prepare a document and present it to Judge Davis so that, if the judge ruled in my favor, my family would not lose all of the assets they have inherited."

A multitude of questions and uncertainty could be heard throughout the courtroom. I pounded my gavel for order and nodded toward Mr. Hamilton.

"Jason, in order to clarify, are we to understand that you are asking your family to forgive you and you're giving them back their entire inheritance, regardless of the outcome of this case?"

Jason's gaze moved to each member of his family in the courtroom as he stated, "Yes. These people are my family, and at the end of this day, no matter the outcome, they will still be my family, and I want them to know I love them, and I want them to have the inheritance my grandfather gave to them."

Everyone sat in stunned silence. Finally, Jason turned to me and spoke.

"Your Honor, can I ask you a question?"

I chuckled and said, "Son, after a year of answering everyone else's questions, I think you're entitled to one."

Jason asked, "Is it true that judges can marry people? I mean can you perform a wedding?"

I laughed aloud and replied, "Son, I haven't married anybody since before you were born, but it doesn't mean I can't do it."

Jason declared, "Well then, sir, if it's agreeable to Alexia, I think we would like you to do the honors as soon as possible."

Alexia rose from her chair at the counsel table, nodding her head vigorously, saying, "Yes. Yes. Yes."

Applause rose from the gallery. I let it die down and then rapped my gavel and declared, "We will address the marriage situation shortly, but first I have a decision to hand down.

"It is the judgment of this court after reviewing each aspect of The Ultimate Gift as set forth in the last will and testament of Howard 'Red' Stevens that Jason Stevens is, indeed, the legal heir of his grandfather's estate and entitled to be awarded with all of his grandfather's assets by this court.

"His earlier motion has been accepted by the court, thus restoring all previously held assets to the Stevens family.

"Jason Stevens, you will have full control of several billion dollars in the Red Stevens Charitable Trust. This court hopes you will act responsibly with it as your grandfather would were he here."

I smiled at Jason and concluded, "And son, after spending more than a year with you here in the courtroom, I don't believe there's a better man anywhere for the job."

———————

That which was the end was also the beginning.

It was only a few days later that I was enjoying a glorious sunrise in the Howard "Red" Stevens Urban Park. I couldn't believe so many people had gathered at that hour. All of the single moms and their kids from the day-care co-op had showed up, along with two busloads of students from the school for the blind. There were numerous wheelchairs and walkers in evidence, demonstrating a great turnout from the senior citizens center. The inner-city kids from the Saturday School were down front, along with many other friends and guests. I recognized the Stevens clan, fully decked out for the occasion. Of course, Theodore J. Hamilton and Margaret Hastings were there, along with Jeffrey Watkins. And, most amazing, was the fact that all of the partners and support staff from the entire legal firm of Dudly, Cheetham, and Leech were there.

Despite the best efforts to keep the media back from the proceedings, many of them had filtered through into the crowd. And standing before me, with as much joy and promise as the sunrise, were Jason and Alexia.

After welcoming everyone and making a few initial statements, I asked, "Jason, do you take Alexia to be your lawfully wedded wife?"

"I do," Jason declared.

"And Alexia," I asked, "do you take Jason to be your lawfully wedded husband?"

She gazed up at him lovingly and promised, "I do."

I concluded, "I now pronounce you husband and wife. You may kiss the bride, and please accept my most sincere wishes for a healthy, happy, and Ultimate Life."

ABOUT THE AUTHOR

Jim Stovall is among the most sought-after motivational speakers anywhere. Despite failing eyesight and eventual blindness, Jim Stovall has been a national champion Olympic weight lifter, a successful investment broker, and an entrepreneur. He is the cofounder and president of the Narrative Television Network, which makes movies and television accessible for America's 13 million blind and visually impaired people and their families. Although NTN was originally designed for the blind and visually impaired, more than 60 percent of its nationwide audience is made up of fully sighted people who simply enjoy the programming. The network's programming is also available free of charge, 24 hours a day, via the Internet at www.NarrativeTV.com.

Jim Stovall hosts the network's talk show, *NTN Showcase*. His guests have included Katharine Hepburn, Jack Lemmon, Carol Channing, Steve Allen, and Eddie Albert, as well as many others. The Narrative Television Network has received an Emmy Award and an International Film and Video Award among its many industry honors. It has grown to include more than 1,200 cable systems and broadcast stations, reaching more than 35 million homes in the United States, and it is shown in eleven foreign countries.

Jim Stovall joined the ranks of Walt Disney, Orson Welles, and four U.S. presidents when he was selected as one of the Ten Outstanding Young Americans by the U.S. Junior Chamber of Commerce in 1994. He has appeared on *Good Morning America* and CNN and has been featured in *Reader's Digest*, *TV Guide*, and

Time magazines. He is the author of previous books titled *You Don't Have to Be Blind to See, Success Secrets of Super Achievers, The Way I See the World,* and the prequel to this book entitled *The Ultimate Gift.* *The Ultimate Gift* has sold in excess of 2 million copies in more than a dozen languages and has been made into a major motion picture starring James Garner, Lee Meriwether, Brian Dennehy, and Abigail Breslin. The President's Committee on Equal Opportunity selected Jim Stovall as the 1997 Entrepreneur of the Year. In June 2000, Jim Stovall joined notables such as President Jimmy Carter, Nancy Reagan, and Mother Teresa when he received the International Humanitarian Award.

Jim Stovall can be reached at 918-627-1000.